James Hadley Chase and The Murder Room

>>> This title is part of The Murder Room, our series dedicated to making available out-of-print or hard-to-find titles by classic crime writers.

Crime fiction has always held up a mirror to society. The Victorians were fascinated by sensational murder and the emerging science of detection; now we are obsessed with the forensic detail of violent death. And no other genre has so captivated and enthralled readers.

Vast troves of classic crime writing have for a long time been unavailable to all but the most dedicated frequenters of second-hand bookshops. The advent of digital publishing means that we are now able to bring you the backlists of a huge range of titles by classic and contemporary crime writers, some of which have been out of print for decades.

From the genteel amateur private eyes of the Golden Age and the femmes fatales of pulp fiction, to the morally ambiguous hard-boiled detectives of mid twentieth-century America and their descendants who walk our twenty-first century streets, The Murder Room has it all. **>>>**

The Murder Room
Where Criminal Minds Meet

themurderroom.com

James Hadley Chase (1906–1985)

Born René Brabazon Raymond in London, the son of a British colonel in the Indian Army, James Hadley Chase was educated at King's School in Rochester, Kent, and left home at the age of 18. He initially worked in book sales until, inspired by the rise of gangster culture during the Depression and by reading James M. Cain's *The Postman Always Rings Twice*, he wrote his first novel, *No Orchids for Miss Blandish*. Despite the American setting of many of his novels, Chase (like Peter Cheyney, another hugely successful British noir writer) never lived there, writing with the aid of maps and a slang dictionary. He had phenomenal success with the novel, which continued unabated throughout his entire career, spanning 45 years and nearly 90 novels. His work was published in dozens of languages and over thirty titles were adapted for film. He served in the RAF during World War II, where he also edited the RAF Journal. In 1956 he moved to France with his wife and son; they later moved to Switzerland, where Chase lived until his death in 1985.

By James Hadley Chase
(published in the Murder Room)

No Orchids for Miss Blandish
  (1939)
Eve (1945)
More Deadly Than the Male
  (1946)
Mission to Venice (1954)
Mission to Siena (1955)
Not Safe to Be Free (1958)
Shock Treatment (1959)
Come Easy – Go Easy (1960)
What's Better Than Money?
  (1960)
Just Another Sucker (1961)
I Would Rather Stay Poor (1962)
A Coffin from Hong Kong
  (1962)
Tell it to the Birds (1963)
One Bright Summer Morning
  (1963)
The Soft Centre (1964)
You Have Yourself a Deal (1966)
Have This One on Me (1967)
Well Now, My Pretty (1967)
Believed Violent (1968)
An Ear to the Ground (1968)
The Whiff of Money (1969)
The Vulture Is a Patient Bird
  (1969)
Like a Hole in the Head (1970)

An Ace Up My Sleeve (1971)
Want to Stay Alive? (1971)
Just a Matter of Time (1972)
You're Dead Without Money
  (1972)
Have a Change of Scene (1973)
Knock, Knock! Who's There?
  (1973)
Goldfish Have No Hiding
  Place (1974)
So What Happens to Me? (1974)
The Joker in the Pack (1975)
Believe This, You'll Believe
  Anything (1975)
Do Me a Favour – Drop Dead
  (1976)
I Hold the Four Aces (1977)
My Laugh Comes Last (1977)
Consider Yourself Dead (1978)
You Must Be Kidding (1979)
A Can of Worms (1979)
Try This One for Size (1980)
You Can Say That Again (1980)
Hand Me a Fig-Leaf (1981)
Have a Nice Night (1982)
We'll Share a Double Funeral
  (1982)
Not My Thing (1983)
Hit Them Where It Hurts (1984)

I Hold the Four Aces

James Hadley Chase

An Orion book

Copyright © Hervey Raymond 1977

The right of James Hadley Chase to be identified as the author of this work has been asserted in accordance with the Copyright, Designs and Patents Act 1988.

This edition published by
The Orion Publishing Group Ltd
Orion House
5 Upper St Martin's Lane
London WC2H 9EA

An Hachette UK company
A CIP catalogue record for this book is available from the British Library

ISBN 978 1 4719 0395 3

www.orionbooks.co.uk

CHAPTER ONE

BEFORE pushing his breakfast tray aside, Jack Archer made sure there was nothing more to eat. He peered into the minute coffee pot, grimaced, then sighing, he lit a Gauloise, and then looked around the sleazy, little hotel bedroom.

He reminded himself that he had been in worse hotels than the Saint Sabin, but not much worse. At least it was clean, and more important, the cheapest hotel in Paris. He checked his wrist watch. It was time he left for his appointment with Joe Patterson. Again he grimaced, thinking of the dreary, complicated journey by Metro to the Plaza Athénée Hotel: Duroc – Invalides – Concorde – Franklin Roosevelt, and finally Alma Marceau. His mind shifted into the past when he would have done this journey in comfort in a Hertz chauffeur-driven car, but that was in the past.

He put on his jacket, then regarded himself in the flyblown mirror. He saw reflected, a tall, heavily-built man, fifty years old, with thinning straw-coloured hair, fleshy jowls, a florid complexion and washed-out blue eyes. He was depressingly aware that his paunch made his jacket hang badly. He was also depressingly aware that his suit, made by one of the best English tailors, was now shapeless and threadbare. All the same, he told himself, as he looked at himself in the mirror, he still made a reasonably impressive figure: shabby, yes, but that air of authority that had served him so well in the past remained.

He looked out of the window. The sun was shining. The narrow street, off Rue de Sèvres, was jammed with slow-moving traffic. The noise of grinding gears and revving engines came through the closed window. He decided not to wear a topcoat which was even shabbier than his suit. He

1

hesitated about taking his hat. Experience had taught him that a hat cost money. He was sure the hat-check girl at the Plaza Athénée Hotel would expect at least a three francs tip. So leaving his hat and picking up his well-worn brief-case, he moved into the long corridor, locked his bedroom door, then began to walk towards the ancient elevator.

A man came from a room by the elevator, locked his door, then thumbed the elevator button.

Looking at him, Archer slowed his stride. This man was at least six foot three inches tall. He was the most impressive male Archer had ever seen: slim, but powerfully-built, with dark brown swept-back hair, a long face, an eagle-like nose and dark penetrating eyes. All this Archer took in at a glance. Apart from this man's impressive handsomeness, and Archer thought he must be a movie star to be this handsome, his clothes made a tremendous impact on Archer. This man's clothes, Archer thought, must have cost a fortune. Although they were casual, they had the cut, that excellence, that revealed impeccable style. The Gucci belt and the Gucci shoes, and the whiter-than-white shirt, gave the impression of wealth, but what really impressed Archer was the unmistakable old Etonian tie. Archer had spent many months in England, and had come to recognize this snob status symbol which he had always envied.

The man entered the elevator cage and was waiting for Archer to join him.

As Archer entered, he caught the smell of an expensive after-shave as the man nodded to him and smiled.

God! Archer thought, what a man! Envy stabbed him. This Adonis, probably in his late thirties, was deeply sun-tanned, and his smile revealed glittering white teeth. Archer was quick to see he was wearing a gold Omega wrist watch and a gold signet ring. On his left wrist he wore a gold and platinum chain bracelet.

'A lovely day,' the man said as Archer closed the elevator door. His voice was low-pitched, deep, musical and sensual. 'Paris in the spring.'

'Yes,' Archer said. He was so off-balance to find a man of

this obvious wealth in this sleazy hotel, he could think of nothing else to say.

His companion produced from his pocket a gold cigarette case with initials set in diamonds.

'I see you are smoking,' he said, and took a cigarette from the case. He then produced a Dunhill gold lighter, also decorated with diamonds. 'It is a terrible habit ... so they say.' He lit the cigarette as the cage descended to the hotel lobby, then nodding to Archer, he crossed to the reception desk, left his key, and walked out into the narrow, busy street.

Archer had been staying at the hotel for the past three weeks and had become friendly with Monsieur Cavelle who acted as reception clerk and concierge. He placed his key on the counter, then asked, 'Who was that gentleman?'

Cavelle, a small, shabby, unhappy-looking man, peered at Archer.

'That was Monsieur Christopher Grenville. He arrived from Germany last night.'

'From Germany? Surely he is English?'

'Yes, Monsieur Archer, he is English.'

'Is he staying here long?'

'He has reserved a room for a week, monsieur.'

Archer switched on his smooth smile.

'He has come at the right time ... spring in Paris,' and nodding, he walked out onto the street.

What in the world, he thought, could a man of Grenville's obvious wealth be doing staying in the cheapest hotel in Paris? That gold cigarette case must be worth at least twenty thousand francs. Most odd! But as soon as he entered the Metro station, he dismissed Grenville and began to think about Joe Patterson and this absurd proposition Patterson was trying to promote.

Eighteen months ago, Archer wouldn't have considered for one moment working for a man like Patterson, but now, as he continually reminded himself, beggars couldn't be choosers.

Sitting in the smelly, jogging second-class compartment of the Metro train, Archer's mind went into the past. Eighteen months ago, he had been a senior partner of a highly reputable firm of international lawyers in Lausanne, Switzerland. He had had Herman Rolfe's Swiss account, and Rolfe had been one of the richest men in the world, nudging shoulders with Getty and the late Onassis. Archer and Rolfe's wife, Helga, had looked after Rolfe's Swiss investments which amounted to some twenty million dollars.

You were too ambitious, Archer told himself, as he let his heavy body roll with the motion of the train, and you were unlucky. His chance to make real money had come from inside information that there was a mine in Australia that was about to strike nickel. He hadn't hesitated. The tip had come from a good friend. The shares were ridiculously low, so he had bought heavily, using Rolfe's money, embezzling over two million dollars with every intention of repaying when the shares jumped, but they didn't jump for there was no nickel. If Helga, Rolfe's wife, had been co-operative, maybe the cards would have fallen right for him, but she hadn't been co-operative.* Archer had expected Rolfe to prosecute, but he hadn't. Archer eventually had realized that Rolfe had discovered that he (Archer) had been Helga's lover. Rolfe had been a man who couldn't face scandal so he hadn't prosecuted, being shrewd enough to know Archer would have told the court of his relations with Helga, but Rolfe had had his revenge. He had blackballed Archer. The word had gone out: don't use this man: a deadly thing.

When Rolfe had withdrawn his account, the firm Archer worked with had folded. The other two partners were elderly and happy to retire. They had given Archer a copper handshake of fifty thousand francs, and Archer had found himself unemployed. At first, he was confident he could carve a new career for himself, but he quickly discovered the power of Rolfe's blackball, even though Rolfe had been dead for the past five months.

No reputable firm wanted him and gradually he had been forced to become a member of the fringe people: the ex-

* See *An Ace Up My Sleeve*.

ploiters, the shifty, the money-hunters, the promotion men who tried to sell what they didn't own.

Archer was not only a brilliant international lawyer and a top-class tax consultant, he also had a smooth bedside manner, and spoke French, German and Italian fluently. But for one greedy, stupid slip-up which had turned him into an embezzler and a forger, he would have had a spectacular future. But he had slipped-up, and now, he was desperately trying to earn something: not even a living, just eating-money.

He had been approached by a South American, Edmondo (call me Ed) Shappilo, who had suggested Archer might be interested to do some legal work for an important promotion company. Archer, with no more than his copper handshake behind him, could scarcely conceal his eagerness, although he was astute enough to guess this legal work could once again fizzle out as other legal work he had done for the shifty had fizzled out. Shappilo, sauve and thin, with long black hair, said the company would be prepared to pay Archer a weekly retainer of one hundred dollars and a one and a half per cent cut on the deal when it jelled. Shappilo talked airily of ten million dollars, and Archer had pricked up his ears. Shappilo went on to say he was representing a wealthy American who had promoted a number of successful property deals, but this particular promotion under discussion was his biggest.

'Mr. Patterson has a genius for supplying a demand and for financing that demand,' Shappilo said, smiling at Archer. 'At this very moment he is negotiating with the Shah of Iran, and the Shah is very, very interested. We would want you to tie up the legal ends and to handle the contracts. We understand this is your kind of work.'

Archer said it was.

Shappilo then gave him a couple of highly-coloured brochures and the details of the proposition, immaculately typed. If, after studying the papers, Shappilo went on, Archer felt he could be helpful, Mr. Patterson, who was staying at the Plaza Athénée Hotel, would like to meet him.

The company to be promoted was to be called 'The Blue

Sky Holiday Camps'. The camps were to be built in various sunspots in Europe. One of the brochures showed individual cabins with thatched roofs, cunningly drawn by an expert artist, showing every kind of play-time facility, a restaurant, a vast swimming pool, and so on and so on. Reading the print, then studying the small print, Archer decided this was nothing new. There were already many such camps dotted around Europe, and he knew, because of the exchange rates, a lot of these camps were in financial trouble, but he was being offered $100 a week and that was eating-money.

Who knows? He thought as he changed trains, heading for Franklin Roosevelt Station, the Shah just might be stupid enough to invest his petrol dollars in a scheme like this, but he doubted it.

He walked into the lobby of the Plaza Athénée Hotel three minutes before 11.00 to find Ed Shappilo waiting for him.

Shappilo didn't smile as he shook hands and Archer's heart sank. Usually, Shappilo had greeted him with a flashing smile, but today, he appeared to be plunged into gloom.

'Something wrong, Ed?' Archer asked uneasily.

'Let us say a set-back,' Shappilo returned, and still grasping Archer's hand, he led him to two chairs in a corner, 'but nothing that can't be rectified. Sit down.' He released Archer's hand and sank into one of the chairs. 'The Shah has turned our promotion down ... most unexpected. It is ridiculous, of course, since he could have made a handsome profit, but he has decided to withdraw.'

Although Archer had expected this, it came as a shock because he saw the $100 a week retainer vanishing before he had received the first payment.

'I am sorry to hear that,' he said.

'Yes, but it is not the end of the world. There are other sources to be tapped. Mr. Patterson would still like to meet you.' Shappilo made a grimace. 'He is not in the best of moods. Just go along with him, Jack. There are times when he can be extremely pleasant, but not this morning.'

Archer regarded Shappilo for a long moment.

'Am I still going to be employed by him, Ed?' he asked.

'I would say yes. After all a hundred dollars a week isn't much.' Shappilo smiled. 'He seems impressed by your qualifications.' He got to his feet. 'Come along. I'm sure you could do with a drink.'

That, Archer thought, as he followed Shappilo along the corridor, was the understatement of the week. He yearned for a drink!

In one of the discreet alcoves, Joe Patterson was drinking his fourth double whisky of the morning.

Patterson was short, bulky with a red face, pitted with old acne scars. His dyed black hair was thinning, his nose bulbous, his eyes small and mean.

Archer saw at once he was slightly drunk. He was one of those Americans Archer detested: loud-voiced, vulgar, loud clothes, and of course the inevitable cigar.

Patterson stared blearily at him, then waved him to a chair by his side.

'So you're Archer, huh?' he said. 'What'll you drink?'

'A gin martini, thank you,' Archer said and sat down. Shappilo snapped his fingers and gave the order while Archer placed his brief-case between his feet and looked at Patterson.

'Ed tells me you've looked at our promotion, Archer,' Patterson said. 'What did you think?'

'I think it would supply a very necessary and popular demand,' Archer said carefully.

'You're goddamn right.' Patterson screwed up his eyes. 'Yeah, that's talking. Then why the hell have these niggers turned it down?'

'There could be several reasons,' Archer said smoothly. 'I wouldn't care to express an opinion, since I wasn't in on the original negotiations.'

Patterson grinned.

'You goddamn lawyers.' He pulled at his cigar and released a cloud of smoke. 'Never get a straight answer.' He leaned forward, poking his cigar at Archer. 'Now, I'll tell you something. Ed is going to Saudi Arabia tomorrow afternoon. Those finks out there are stinking with money. Never mind Iran. We'll get the money from these other finks. How's about you going with Ed and fixing the legal end?'

The idea of Shappilo getting near a minister of importance in Saudi Arabia to promote such an obvious lemon as the Blue Sky Holiday Camps was so ludicrous that Archer nearly laughed, but he kept thinking of the $100 a week, so he pretended to think, then nodded.

'Yes. I would be prepared to accompany Mr. Shappilo.' He paused, then went on, without much confidence, 'But not at $100 a week retainer, Mr. Patterson.'

Patterson squinted at him.

'Who said you would? You take this trip, and I'll pay your expenses. You get a two per cent cut when you two bring back the contract. That's worth real money, Archer.'

How many times, Archer thought, had he heard this kind of talk? Always in millions: always so much percentage.

'Have you any introductions out there?' he asked.

Patterson finished his drink, then looked at Shappilo.

'You fixed any introductions, Ed?'

Shappilo examined his fingernails.

'Well, no. The Paris finks are difficult. I think we will make real progress on the spot, rather than fool around with the Embassy here.'

Patterson nodded.

'Yeah. Go out there and fix something.' He lifted his empty glass. 'Get me a refill, Ed.'

While Shappilo was snapping his fingers, Archer had a moment to think. At least he would get a free trip to the Middle East. This cheered him a little. Who knows? He might pick up some lucrative work out there, drop Shappilo and settle in Saudi Arabia for a while. Who knows?

As the waiter brought Patterson's drink, there was a slight commotion along the corridor that led to the elevators.

A woman and two men, accompanied by the assistant manager of the hotel, followed by two porters wheeling hand-trucks piled high with expensive-looking luggage, came down the corridor.

Archer's heart skipped a beat as he recognized the woman.

8

Helga Rolfe for God's sake!

He hadn't seen Helga since they had parted after his abortive attempt to blackmail her to conceal his embezzlement from her husband. Hurriedly, he raised his hand to shield his face. He didn't want her to see him.

He felt a pang of frustrated envy as he watched her stride down the corridor. She looked wonderful! Wearing a pale beige suède coat, her blonde hair silky and glittering, her head held high, she conveyed a picture of confident wealth.

Her two companions kept pace with her. The taller of the two, bent a little to talk, while the shorter man seemed to be having trouble in keeping up.

The little procession disappeared into the waiting elevator and was whisked out of sight.

'That's some doll,' Patterson said. 'Who could she be?'

Here was the opportunity to impress this vulgar American, Archer thought.

'That was Madame Helga Rolfe,' he said.

Patterson squinted at him.

'Rolfe? You mean *the* Rolfe? The electronics man?'

'Yes, but Rolfe died a few months ago.' Archer sipped his martini. 'Helga is now in charge of the corporation, and appears to be handling it well.' He said this carelessly as a throw-away.

Patterson's mean little eyes opened wide.

'Is that right? Who were the two finks with her?'

Archer leaned back and took out his pack of Gauloises.

'Here, have a man's smoke, for God's sake.' Patterson produced a cigar in a metal container.

'Thanks, I will.' While Archer removed the cigar from the container, he went on, 'The taller man is Stanley Winborn, head of Rolfe's legal department. The short, fat man is the Vice-president, Frederick Loman.' He lit the cigar and puffed smoke. 'I suppose the corporation now is worth over a billion dollars. I know for a fact, Helga's personal fortune is worth at least a hundred million.'

Patterson sucked in his breath.

'Hell! That's real money!'

'You could say that.' Archer smiled. He finished his drink and set down his empty glass.

'Get him another drink, Ed,' Patterson said.

While Shappilo was snapping his fingers at a waiter, Patterson went on, 'Sounds as if you know the doll.'

This was the moment when Archer should have kept his mouth shut, but the martini, after a miserable dinner the previous night, and a still more miserable breakfast, had made him slightly drunk.

'Know her? Not so long ago, she and I handled Rolfe's Swiss business, and not so long ago we were intimate friends,' and he winked.

'For Pete's sake!' Patterson was obviously impressed. 'You mean you screwed her?'

Archer accepted the martini the waiter offered him.

'Let us say we were intimate,' he said.

'Yeah. I get the photo.' Patterson pulled at his cigar. 'Well, what do you know?' He scratched his bulbous nose, then went on, 'So she's worth a hundred million?'

'About that.' Archer drank half his martini. He was now feeling very relaxed.

'But you're not working with her any more?' The small eyes probed.

Careful, Archer told himself, you're letting your tongue run away.

'We had a falling-out. She's very difficult. I found I couldn't work with her any more.' He sipped his drink. 'I take it, Ed will arrange the air tickets to Saudi Arabia? I just wait for instructions?'

Patterson thought for a long moment, finished his drink, then shook his head.

'Why the hell should we go to these Arab finks for money when it is sitting right here in this goddamn hotel?'

Archer stared at him.

'I don't follow you, Mr. Patterson. In this hotel?'

Patterson leaned forward and tapped Archer on his knee.

'Use your head, Archer. With your contact with this Rolfe doll, it will be a cinch for you to sell our promotion to her.

We want a couple of million. That's chickfeed to her. Put it to her. Okay?'

Archer's hands turned clammy.

'I assure you, Mr. Patterson, Madame Rolfe wouldn't think of investing money in holiday camps. I know her too well. No . . . it just wouldn't work.'

Patterson stared at him for a long moment, his mean little eyes probing, then he looked at Shappilo.

'Where's the goddamn grillroom? I want to put on the feed-bag.' He got to his feet as Shappilo pointed down the long corridor. Looking at Archer, Patterson went on, 'Now listen: talk to this Rolfe doll and set her up for me. All I want from you is to set up a meeting. I'll do the selling. And listen, Archer, I hire successful men. You fix it for me to meet her or you don't come on my pay roll.' He walked off down the corridor.

Shappilo got to his feet.

'You heard what the man said, Jack. It shouldn't be all that tricky, you knowing her so well. Well, let's hope we meet again,' and he followed Patterson to the grillroom leaving Archer staring bleakly after him.

Back in his hotel bedroom, after a sandwich lunch, Archer cursed himself for boasting to Patterson about his association with Helga. He must be getting old! he thought. A year ago, he would never have done such a thing. What to do now?

He had checked through his remaining traveller's cheques. His money was running out. There were no other irons in the fire: no other promotions, no other offers for legal work. And yet, he knew it would be impossible to approach Helga.

The last time they had been together, she had threatened him with a ten year jail sentence! He imagined how she would react if he suggested she should meet a man like Joe Patterson . . . It was unthinkable!

So what to do?

He took off his jacket, hung it in the closet, then stretched out on the lumpy bed. He did his best thinking when completely relaxed. The martinis he had drunk now had their effect and he drifted off into a heavy sleep. He woke to find the room in semi-darkness. He must have slept for more than three hours, he thought, then he became aware that someone was knocking on his door.

Looking at his watch, he saw the time was 18.20. Probably the maid, he thought irritably, and called to come in, at the same time switching on the light.

The door opened and Christopher Grenville, in all his finery, stood in the doorway.

Startled, Archer gaped at him, then hastily swung his feet to the floor.

'I am afraid I have disturbed you,' Grenville said in his deep, musical voice. 'I'm terribly sorry.'

'Not at all ... not at all.' Archer smoothed down his ruffled, thinning hair.

'Stupid of me, but I've run out of cigarettes,' Grenville went on. 'I wonder if I could cadge a couple from you ... such a bore to have to walk all the way to the tabac.'

Archer was staring at this Adonis, and an idea suddenly dropped into his fertile mind. He got to his feet, picked up his pack of Gauloises and offered it.

'I am always doing the same thing,' he said, and smiled pleasantly. 'My name's Jack Archer. You're English, I believe?'

'Terribly English. Christopher Grenville. Can I take two? I see you haven't many left.'

Archer's eyes went over the immaculate clothes, the shoes, the platinum and gold bracelet.

'Go ahead. I was just taking a rest. I've had a trying morning. If you have nothing better to do ... why not sit down?'

'I don't want to be in the way.' Grenville sank into the creaky armchair. 'Quaint little hotel, isn't it?'

'You could say that, but it's convenient.'

Grenville laughed: an easy, musical laugh.

'Let us say it is cheap.'

Archer eyed him. Grenville appeared to be completely relaxed and friendly.

'Without doubt this is the cheapest hotel in Paris,' Archer said.

'I know. I make a study of hotels: that's why I am here.'

Archer raised his eyebrows.

'Then your appearance is extremely deceptive, Mr. Grenville.'

Grenville laughed again.

'Appearances generally are. For all I know, you are an eccentric millionaire.'

'I wish I was.' Archer sighed. 'I am an international lawyer. If I may ask, what is your line?'

Grenville stretched out his long legs and regarded his glittering Gucci shoes.

'You could say I am an opportunist. Right at this moment I am looking for an opportunity. The world is my oyster.'

An opportunist? Archer thought as he tapped ash off his cigarette. That was an admirable description of himself.

A little tartly, he said, 'You appear well-equipped. Have you any irons in the fire?'

'You mean my trappings?' Grenville fingered his gold and platinum bracelet. 'Every successful opportunist must have trappings. Once he becomes shabby, there is little hope for him.'

Archer accepted the truth, but it hurt. He winced.

'I agree, but you haven't answered my question.'

'Irons in the fire? Not right now, but who knows? Tomorrow is another day. An opportunist has to live on hope.'

Archer regarded the handsome face, the immaculate clothes, the easy, friendly smile. Handled right, he told himself, this man could solve his problem with Patterson.

'I might be able to put something interesting your way,' he said cautiously.

'I am always interested in anything interesting,' Grenville said. 'Suppose we leave this dismal room and share a plate of spaghetti together?' His smile broadened. 'I haven't eaten all day, and the thing I call my brain doesn't function too well on an empty stomach.'

Archer was almost sure this was his man. He got to his feet.

'We'll do better than that. I'll buy you a steak dinner. Let's go.'

An hour later, the two men pushed aside their plates and sat back in the shabby bistro, after eating two tough steaks with french fried and canned peas. Archer noticed Grenville had eaten as if he hadn't had a meal for some days. Grenville had kept up a monologue in his musical baritone voice, expressing his opinions about the world's politics, art in Paris, and books. His voice had a hypnotic effect on Archer who was content to listen, surprised by Grenville's wide range of knowledge.

'That was very acceptable,' Grenville said, laying down his knife and fork. 'Now to business. What is this something interesting you spoke about?'

Archer sat back and reached for a toothpick.

'I think it is possible that you and I could work profitably together, but first, I would like to know more about you. You call yourself an opportunist. Just what does that mean?'

'I wonder if your budget would run to some cheese?' Grenville asked. 'It seems a pity not to finish with cheese.'

'The budget does not run to anything except coffee,' Archer said firmly.

'Then let us settle for coffee.' Grenville smiled. 'Suppose you give me some idea what is in your mind before I lay my soul bare?'

'Yes ... fair enough.' Archer ordered two coffees. 'I am handling the legal end of an important promotion. The promoter is an American who is trying to raise money to finance a number of holiday camps in the sun spots of Europe. He needs around two million dollars. He is a rough diamond, but I think I could persuade him to employ you as his front man. The idea has only just occurred to me so I must talk to him. I have a feeling he would be interested. I am sure your appearance would impress him, but I must have some information about you before I approach him ... so over to you.'

Grenville sipped his coffee and grimaced.

'I can now imagine what acorn coffee was like during the war,' he said, then looking at Archer, his dark eyes thoughtful, he went on, 'Aren't holiday camps rather old hat these days with the currency rates as they are?'

Archer nodded approval. This man was nobody's fool.

'We'll go into that later. Suppose you tell me about yourself.'

Grenville opened his gold cigarette case, found it empty, frowned, then looked inquiringly at Archer.

'Have you any cigarettes left or are we to be smokeless?'

Archer signalled to the waiter and asked for a pack of Gauloises. When they had lit up, Archer said, 'The ball is now in your court, Grenville.'

Grenville gave his charming smile.

'I'm Chris to my friends ... so call me Chris. Yes ... the ball. Frankly, I am what is known as a gigolo: a male escort. It is a despised profession, but make no mistake about it, it is a profession. It is despised by those who don't understand the very urgent need elderly women have for male company. Go to any good hotel and you will find elderly women boring barmen, boring waiters, looking hopefully for an unattached male. There are thousands of rich, fat or scraggy, unattractive, dull, neurotic, lonely women who crave to have a last fling, to be taken around and be pampered and who pay good money for the attention. I am one of those who supply this demand. These trappings you have remarked on are gifts from old, frustrated women. This bracelet was given to me by a poor old thing who imagined I was in love with her. The cigarette case came from a fat Austrian countess who insisted that I should dance with her every night for three dreadful weeks. Fortunately for me, and unfortunately for her, she suffered a minor stroke or else, I suppose, I would be dancing with her now. I am thirty-nine years of age. For the past twenty years I have been making the lives of elderly women happy.' He finished his coffee and smiled at Archer. 'There, Jack, you have it in a nutshell.'

A surge of triumph ran through Archer. He hadn't mistaken his man!

'I think we will have some cheese,' he said.

The hands of the clock above the concierge's desk moved to midnight as Joe Patterson entered the lobby of the Plaza Athénée Hotel. He paused at the desk to pick up his key as Archer approached.

'Good evening, Mr. Patterson.'

Scowling, Patterson turned, then seeing Archer, who had been waiting in the lobby for the past two hours, he snapped, 'What do you want?'

'I have something important to discuss with you, Mr. Patterson,' Archer said smoothly, 'but if it's the wrong time . . .'

'Okay, okay. I've just been with a chick, and boy! did she give out! Come on, let's get a goddamn drink.'

Archer followed Patterson to an alcove, waited until the waiter had served the drinks and while Patterson lit a cigar.

'You been busy, Archer? How's about the Rolfe doll?'

'It is more than possible,' Archer said, 'that Madame Rolfe can be persuaded to finance Blue Sky.'

Patterson squinted at him.

'Have you talked to her? You said this morning she wouldn't touch it.'

'That was first thoughts, Mr. Patterson. Since then, I have had second thoughts. I now believe she could be persuaded.'

Patterson grinned.

'Yeah. Nothing like second thoughts. Have you contacted her?'

'The set-up is complex, Mr. Patterson. No, I haven't contacted her and I don't intend to, but nevertheless, I am satisfied she can be persuaded to invest two million dollars in your promotion.'

Patterson scowled at him.

'Cut the double-talk, Archer! What the hell do you mean?'

'For you to understand the situation, Mr. Patterson, it is necessary for you to know that Helga Rolfe is a nymphomaniac,' Archer said.

Patterson gaped at him.

'A nympho ... what?'

'A woman who has a compulsive need for a man.'

Patterson's little eyes opened wide.

'You mean she has hot pants?'

'A little more than that, Mr. Patterson. I have known Helga for the past twenty years. Sex is as necessary to her as food is to you.'

Patterson was intrigued. He took a pull at his drink, knocked cigar ash on the floor and leered at Archer.

'Well! She's a doll too! You think she and I could get together in bed? If I gave it to her, she would part with the dough?'

Archer regarded the pock-marked, sweaty, coarse face. If only we could see ourselves as others see us, he thought.

'I think not, Mr. Patterson,' he said, picking his words carefully. 'Helga seems only interested in rather special, unusual men. She likes them tall, younger than herself, extremely handsome, witty, preferably with a knowledge of the arts, and of course, since she speaks German, French and Italian fluently she would expect the man to do the same.'

Patterson chewed his cigar.

'Jesus! For a doll with hot pants she sounds hard to please.'

'She is worth a hundred million,' Archer said, and smiled. 'She can afford to be difficult.'

'Yeah.' Patterson began to pick his nose. 'How's about Ed Shappilo? He looks good and he speaks Spanish. How's about him?'

Archer sadly shook his head.

'I don't think Ed is quite in the same bracket as Helga Rolfe, Mr. Patterson. My idea is this: let us suppose we find the ideal man. He meets Helga who falls in love with him. I know Helga. Once she falls for a man, she will do anything for him. After a week or so, this man explains the Blue Sky promotion to her, asking her advice. He tells her he is acting for you. What does she think? Helga, in love, can be very generous. As you have so rightly said, two million is chickfeed to her. This man then tells her unless he can raise the money he will be out of a job. All this will have to be done very subtly. I will handle it, as I know Helga. She will produce the money ... I can practically guarantee it.'

Patterson left his nose alone and sat back, screwing up his eyes while Archer watched him anxiously. Had he handled this right? he asked himself. Everything depended now on how this fat, sweaty man would react.

The long pause while Patterson brooded made Archer sweat. Finally, Patterson nodded.

'Sounds okay. Yeah, I get the photo. You've come up with a smart idea, Archer. I guess I'll have to look around for some stooge to go after her. That ain't going to be easy.'

Archer relaxed. Taking out his handkerchief, he wiped off his hands.

'I wouldn't be here at this hour, Mr. Patterson, with this idea, unless I had already found the right man,' he said. 'After all, that is what you are paying me for – to give you advice and service.'

Patterson sat upright.

'You've found him?'

'The perfect man for Helga,' Archer said. 'She will find him irresistible.'

'For Pete's sake! How did you find him?'

Archer was prepared for this question and had discussed it with Grenville.

'He is a professional gigolo, Mr. Patterson: very high-class and he is used to dealing with middle-aged and elderly, rich women. Some years ago, he looked after an old client of mine and I got to know him. We met by chance this afternoon. As soon as I saw him, I knew I had the solution to our problem. I would like you to meet him, and see for yourself.'

Patterson, scowling, began to pick his nose again.

'A gigolo? Hell! I hate those finks.' Releasing his nose, he rubbed his hand over his sweaty face, then went on, 'You think he can handle the Rolfe doll?'

'I know he can. I wouldn't be here wasting your time unless I was sure,' Archer said.

Patterson thought for a moment, then shrugged.

'Yeah. This could be a smart idea. Okay, tell him to be here tomorrow at eleven.'

Grenville had been very emphatic when and where he was to meet Patterson.

'Even if this man doesn't want me, let us, at least, get a decent lunch out of him,' he had said to Archer. 'Tell him the Ritz grill at one or I don't play.'

'I think it would be unwise, Mr. Patterson, for him to be seen here with you,' Archer said. 'Madame Rolfe might see you two together. My man appears to be occupied, but he could meet us at the Ritz grillroom at one o'clock tomorrow.'

'Who the hell cares if he is occupied or not?' Patterson snarled. 'I'm hiring him, ain't I?'

'That we don't know as yet. This man is very high-class, Mr. Patterson. He has many irons in the fire. If you could make an exception, I suggest it would be profitable for you to meet him as arranged.'

'A goddamn gigolo!'

'They have their uses, Mr. Patterson,' Archer said mildly. 'When he has persuaded Madame Rolfe to part with two million dollars, I think you will agree.'

Patterson stubbed out his cigar, then got to his feet.

'Okay ... the Ritz grill.' He patted Archer on his shoulder. 'You're doing all right, Archer.' He took out his wallet and produced a hundred dollar bill. 'Here .. go, buy yourself a drink.'

As Archer's fingers closed over the bill, Patterson, slightly unsteady, stumped off down the corridor to the elevator.

Seated at a corner table in l'Espadon grillroom of the Ritz Hotel, with Patterson at his side, Archer watched Grenville make his entrance.

'Here he is, Mr. Patterson,' Archer said.

Grenville had kept them waiting a quarter of an hour, and Patterson was now in an ugly mood.

'Who the hell does he think he is?' he kept muttering as the minutes ticked away. 'A goddamn gigolo!'

But Grenville's entrance impressed him. Wearing an immaculate beige-coloured suit, Grenville paused at the entrance: nonchalant, confident, and imposingly handsome.

The maitre d'hôtel hurried towards him.

'Monsieur Grenville! This is a pleasure! You have been deserting us!'

As this was in French, Patterson squinted at Archer.

'What's he say?'

'The maitre d'hôtel says it is a pleasure to see Mr. Grenville again,' Archer told him.

'Is that right? The fink didn't say that to me!'

Patterson watched Grenville shake hands with the maitre d'hôtel, and then talk briefly; then the maitre d'hôtel conducted him towards Patterson's table. On the way Grenville paused as an elderly waiter, fat, balding, bowed to him.

'Why, Henri, I thought you had retired,' he said and shook hands.

'Hell!' Patterson muttered, obviously impressed. 'This guy seems to be known here.'

'And is known at all the most important restaurants in Paris,' Archer said, delighted by the way Grenville was making his entrance. 'I told you, Mr. Patterson, he is very high-class.'

Grenville reached their table.

'Hello, Jack,' he said, smiling at Archer, then he turned to Patterson. 'You will be Mr. Patterson. I am Grenville.'

Patterson stared up at him, his mean little eyes probing. Archer was scared that Patterson was going to be difficult, but obviously, Grenville's smooth, forcible personality had made an impact.

'Yeah. Archer has been telling me about you.'

There was a waiter to pull out Grenville's chair and he settled at the table.

'It is over a year since I have been here,' Grenville said. 'I have many happy memories of this great hotel.'

The wine waiter was at his elbow.

'Your usual, Mr. Grenville?'

Grenville nodded as Patterson gaped. The wine waiter

went away and the maitre d'hôtel arrived with the menus.

Grenville waved to Patterson.

'Mr. Patterson is our host, Jacques,' he said. 'Remember him. He is influential and important.'

'Certainly, Mr. Grenville,' and the maitre d'hôtel darted around the table and handed Patterson the menu. Thrown off his stride, Patterson stared at the menu which, being in French, he couldn't read, then growled, 'I'll take onion soup and a rare steak.'

Grenville's martini arrived. He sipped and nodded his approval.

'Absolutely right, Charles.'

'And what would you like, Monsieur Grenville?' the maitre d'hôtel asked, hovering over Grenville like a mother hen over her chick.

Grenville didn't consult the menu.

'The *langoustine*, Louis?'

'Impeccable, monsieur.'

'Then why not the *gratin de langoustine* and the *caneton en cocotte*?'

'An excellent choice, Monsieur Grenville.'

Grenville looked at Archer.

'I suggest you take the same, Jack. It is extremely good.'

Archer, who was famished, nodded eagerly.

The maitre d'hôtel left them.

Grenville turned his flashing smile on Patterson.

'Jack has explained the situation, Mr. Patterson, and I find it interesting. I suggest we go into details after lunch. It would be a pity to discuss business while we eat.' He gave his baritone, musical laugh. 'Pleasure before work.' Then without giving Patterson a chance to say anything, he launched into a steady monologue about the history of the Ritz Hotel, mentioning great names as if he knew the people and adding two amusing anecdotes about eccentric visitors while Patterson, bewildered, could only sit and stare.

The onion soup and the *gratin de langoustine* arrived and the wine waiter appeared at Grenville's elbow.

'Mr. Patterson is the host, Charles,' Grenville said. 'The

cellar here, Mr. Patterson, is still remarkable. If you haven't tried the Muscadet 1929, you should, and I believe they still have a few bottles of Margaux '59.' He looked at the wine waiter. 'Do you, Charles?'

The wine waiter beamed.

'For you, Monsieur Grenville.'

Patterson, who knew nothing about wine, was overawed. He nodded.

'Okay, so we have that,' he said.

During the impeccable meal, Grenville talked. He began by advising Patterson to see a new collection of modern paintings at a little gallery on the Left Bank.

'There are two moderns that will be worth money in a couple of years,' he said. 'Cracinella: unknown at the moment, but could be as great as Picasso. You could treble your money.' From art, he shifted to music, asking the bewildered Patterson if he had heard of a young pianist, Skalinski, who was quite remarkable.

Patterson ate, grunted and remained bewildered while Archer ate with enjoyment and was delighted with Grenville's performance.

From modern art and music, Grenville went on to talk about films.

'Paris is the showcase of modern movies,' he said as he finished the duck. 'I suppose you don't have time to go to the movies. A man of your stature should take a look at this modern stuff.'

Archer could see that Patterson now was reacting to Grenville's smooth and continuous talk. Grenville never gave Patterson a chance to make any comment. His steady monologue continued while he was served a champagne sorbet which both Patterson and Archer refused. The meal finished, and coffee served, Grenville beckoned to the wine waiter.

'Have you still that favourite of mine, Charles?'

'Certainly, Monsieur Grenville.'

Smiling, Grenville looked at Patterson.

'This is a must, Mr. Patterson: a 1906 cognac. Quite remarkable.'

'I'll take a double whisky,' Patterson grunted, asserting himself.

Grenville looked at Archer who said he would like the cognac. He realized these were the first words he had uttered since Grenville had arrived.

The whisky and the two cognacs were served, then Grenville lit a cigarette, letting Patterson have a good view of the diamond-encrusted gold cigarette case.

'I won't offer you one of these, Mr. Patterson,' he said as he produced his gold lighter. 'I am sure you are a cigar man.'

'You're goddamn right,' Patterson said and lit a cigar.

Archer accepted a cigarette that Grenville offered. He was happily aware that Grenville had Patterson mesmerized the way a skilful matador, with a flick of his cape, mesmerizes a bull. Grenville, with his know-how, his monologue, his influence with the maitre d'hôtel and the waiters, had struck at Patterson's hidden inferiority complex: a complex many Americans suffer from when in Europe.

'Now, Mr. Patterson, let us talk business,' Grenville said, relaxing back in his chair. 'You will, of course, want to know what you are buying. Let me tell you briefly about myself. I am thirty-nine years of age. English, educated at Eton and Cambridge. I speak German, French and Italian fluently. I have played tennis with Rod Laver, and I have played golf in the Amateur Open Golf championship. I ski and water-ski, and I fence. I play the piano rather well and I sing; I have had minor roles at the Scala. I ride and play polo. I understand modern art which interests me. When I left Cambridge, my father wished me to become a very junior partner in his business. This didn't appeal to me.' Grenville smiled. 'I found I could have much more fun looking after elderly rich women. I have this talent for making women happy. I have been a professional gigolo for the past twenty years, and with considerable success. Jack tells me you are looking for an expert like myself to take care of Helga Rolfe. I haven't met the lady, but I am confident I can handle her. You want two million dollars from her to promote a property deal. If you and I can come to an arrangement, I can assure you, I can get this money for you.'

Patterson pulled at his cigar as he stared at Grenville.

'Maybe. Yeah . . . you just might.'

Grenville signalled to the waiter to refill his coffee cup.

'There is no just might, Mr. Patterson, I deliver.'

Patterson brooded for a long minute while Archer watched him anxiously, then Patterson nodded.

'Yeah. Okay. How do you set about it?'

'That you must leave to me,' Grenville said. 'It will take a couple of weeks, but you will get the money.'

Patterson looked questioningly at Archer who nodded.

'I assure you, Mr. Patterson, Chris is as good as his word,' he said.

Patterson grunted.

'Well, okay . . . go ahead.'

Grenville sipped his coffee, then said, 'Naturally, there are conditions on my side. I take it you are prepared to finance me while I take care of Madame Rolfe?'

Patterson stiffened.

'What's that mean?'

'To meet Madame Rolfe on equal terms, I intend to take a suite at the Plaza Athénée. I need to hire an impressive car. I will need five thousand francs for spending money.' Grenville smiled at Patterson. 'I take it you will take care of the bills?'

Giving Patterson no time to think, Archer said smoothly, 'That won't be an excessive outlay for two million dollars, Mr. Patterson. After all, you were prepared to pay the air fare for Ed and myself to Saudi Arabia and all expenses.'

Patterson rolled his cigar around in his mouth while he thought.

'Yeah,' he said finally. 'Okay, but now listen, Grenville, you produce or you're in trouble. I'll stake you, but you deliver!'

Grenville's handsome face turned to stone.

'Mr. Patterson!' There was a bite in his voice. 'Let me remind you that you are not dealing with one of your fellow-countrymen. I understand that you business men like to act tough, now and then. It is part of your business façade, but I will not tolerate anyone threatening me as you have just threatened me. Let that be understood. I have told you I will get two million dollars from Madame Rolfe for your promotion, but on my terms. If you have no confidence in me, now is the time to say so, but never, never threaten me, Mr. Patterson.' He leaned forward and stared directly at Patterson. 'Is that understood?'

Patterson's little eyes shifted.

'Okay, okay. You don't have to blow your cork. Yeah, I understand. Sure . . . forget what I said.'

Archer, who had come out in a cold sweat, relaxed.

'Then please arrange the financial details with Jack. I expect to have five thousand francs by the time I move into the Plaza,' Grenville said. 'I now have an appointment.' He rose to his feet as a waiter snatched away his chair. 'Thank you for the lunch, Mr. Patterson, and good day to you.'

The maitre d'hôtel came hurrying up.

'I trust you were pleased, Monsieur Grenville.'

'A perfect meal, Jacques.' Grenville shook hands, then accompanied by the maitre d'hôtel, he walked out of the grill-room.

'Jesus!' Patterson exclaimed. 'That guy really has class.'

'If anyone can produce two million dollars for you, Mr. Patterson, he will,' Archer said.

'Yeah.' Patterson called for the check. 'He's got real style. Yeah. I don't think this guy can miss.'

As Patterson stared with unbelieving eyes at the amount the lunch had cost, Archer thought, 'I hope to God he doesn't.'

CHAPTER TWO

HELGA ROLFE, one of the richest women in the world, lay in a hot, scented bath in her Plaza Athénée Hotel suite. Her long legs stirred the water and her hands cupped her firm breasts.

Even though she had always travelled V.I.P., and was cosseted by the air hostesses, Helga detested long-distance flights, more particularly when she had to fly in the company of Stanley Winborn whom she disliked and Frederick Loman whom she considered an old bore, but both these men were essential to the smooth running of the Rolfe Electronic Corporation.

There had been a time, when she had become President of the corporation, when she had played with the idea of getting rid of both men, but after considerable thought, she had been forced to accept the fact that these two men were too efficient to lose.

It had been Loman's idea to set up a branch of the Electronic Corporation in France. He had had talks with the French Prime Minister who had been encouraging. The advantages were many, and Helga had agreed. Loman had said he and Winborn would fly over and have further talks.

Springtime in Paris! Helga thought.

To the surprise of the two men, she said she would go with them.

But now, lying in the bath, relaxing after the seven dreary hours of flight, Helga wondered if this had been such a good idea.

Paris in the spring had sounded wonderful, but when you were on your own, when you only had two hard-headed, dreary business men to escort you around, and when you

26

knew the French press was watching, maybe it wasn't such a good idea.

She moved her long, beautiful legs, stirring the water. She had been a widow now for five months. The magic key of Herman Rolfe's millions was hers. She was now worth a hundred million dollars in her own right. She owned a de luxe house in Paradise City, a de luxe penthouse in New York and a de luxe villa in Switzerland. But freedom? Whatever she did was reported in the press. God! How she hated newspapers!

Sex to her was as compulsive as drink to an alcoholic. When Rolfe had died, she had imagined she would be free to have any man who appealed to her, but she quickly discovered that if she wished to avoid newspaper headlines, she still had to be as furtive in her love affairs as she had been when Rolfe had been alive.

During the five months of her so-called freedom, she had had three lovers: a waiter in a New York hotel, an old roué who no one would have suspected was still potent, and a young, smelly hippy to whom she had given a lift, and who had taken her violently in the back of her car.

This can't go on, she told herself. I have all the money in the world. I have everything, but sex. I must find a husband: some wonderful man who will love me, who will be on hand when I get this desperate sex urge so I don't have to be furtive ever again. This is the solution: the only solution.

She got out of the bath and stood before the long mirror and looked at herself. She was now forty-four years of age. Age had been kind to her: expert handling by beauticians and a strict diet. She saw a woman with cone-shaped breasts, a slim body, rounded hips; blonde, with big blue eyes, high cheekbones, full lips and a perfect complexion. She looked ten years younger than she was.

But what was the good of that? she thought bitterly as she began to dry herself. To look like this, to have a body like this without a man to appreciate what she had to offer.

Returning to her suite, she found the maid had unpacked her clothes and everything was in order. She had agreed

(God! What a bore!) to dine with Loman and Winborn in the grillroom. She put on a black silk jersey dress, snatched up a black ostrich feather stole and took the elevator to the ground floor where she found Loman and Winborn waiting.

The two men converged on her. It was now 21.30 and Winborn suggested they had their cocktails at the table. Helga was aware that people were staring as she made her entrance. There was a fat, acne-scarred man, obviously a brash American, who was eating alone, and who stared more than the others.

Patterson watched her as she sat at a table across from him and he nodded to himself. Archer was right! This doll really needed special handling. While he ate yet another steak, he kept watching Helga as she talked to her two companions, and he told himself that Grenville was the right man to cope with this woman.

His meal finished, Patterson toyed with a double whisky on the rocks until Helga and her two escorts left the grillroom. The time now was 22.15, then he wandered into the lobby in time to see Winborn and Loman escorting Helga to the elevator.

As Helga was whisked up to her suite, she thought: 'Once again! Two sleeping pills! Will I ever be free to do what I want?'

Entering her suite, she went to the window and drew aside the heavy drapes. She stared down at the fast-moving traffic. There below her was the excitement of Paris: movement, lights, noise, people. But what can a woman do on her own?

She jerked the drapes together, then turned and looked around the large, lonely suite.

A husband!

That was her solution!

A husband!

She stripped off her clothes and walked naked into the bathroom. She opened the cabinet door and found her sleeping pills. She swallowed two, then paused to look at herself in the mirror.

So this was to be her first night in Paris in the spring!

Going to her bedroom, she put on a shortie nightdress, then flopped into bed. How many times had she done this? Sleeping pills instead of a lover?

A husband, she thought, as the pills began to work. Yes, that was the solution: a kind, marvellous lover!

She drifted away into a drugged sleep.

There was a press photographer lurking outside the hotel as Helga walked into the mid-morning sunshine. Although she hated this ratty-looking little man, she gave him a flashing smile and a wave of her hand as he took her photograph. She had long learned always to be friendly with the press.

She walked up avenue Marceau, crossed to rue Quentin and taking her time, savouring the atmosphere of Paris, arrived at Fouquet's bar and restaurant on avenue Champs-Elysées.

Yes, she thought, this is really Paris in the spring. The chestnut trees were in blossom, crowds of tourists moved up and down the broad sidewalk, the sun shone and the tables of the many cafés were crowded.

She sat down at an unoccupied table and a waiter arrived. She decided to have a late lunch, so she asked for a vodka martini. The waiter, impressed by her champagne-coloured fine wool coat with fur cuffs, came back quickly with the drink.

She sat relaxing, watching the various freaks, the dull-looking tourists, the aged American women in their awful hats and their bejewelled spectacles. It was a panorama that amused her.

Winborn had suggested they should have lunch together, but Helga, rather than share his company again, had said she had shopping to do. She told herself even a meal on her own would be preferable to listening to Winborn's dull utterances.

But a meal on her own in Paris in springtime!

She opened her handbag and took out her cigarette case. As she put the cigarette between her lips, she heard a little

29

click and saw the flame from a diamond-encrusted gold ciga-rette lighter being offered. She dipped the cigarette into the flame, and then looked up.

She wasn't to know that Grenville had been waiting out-side her hotel for nearly an hour, that he had followed her up avenue Marceau and had watched her sit at the table, and then had moved unobtrusively to a table next to hers.

Helga looked into the brown eyes of a man who sent an immediate hot wave of desire through her. This was a man! Everything about him was immaculate: his cream-coloured suit, the black-and-blue tie, the gold and platinum bracelet on his powerful, hairy wrist, and the smile, showing white, perfect teeth.

They looked at each other.

'Springtime in Paris,' Grenville said in his deep, musical voice. 'Everyone raves about it, but when one is alone, it can be a bore.'

'But surely you are not alone?' Helga asked.

'May I put the same question to you?'

She smiled.

'You can, and I am.'

'That's perfect. So we are no longer alone.'

She laughed. For years now she had picked up interesting men and had often regretted it, but the drink, the sunshine, the atmosphere of Paris made her reckless.

'I haven't been to Paris for a year. It doesn't seem to have changed,' she said.

'Can time stand still?' Grenville shrugged. 'Paris has changed. Everything changes. Look at these people.' He waved to the continuous stream of tourists. 'I now have the feeling that people like you and me are fast becoming an-achronistic. It is these people, parading before us in their shabby clothes, their long, dirty hair, their guitars, who will eventually take over the world. People like us with taste, who know the difference between good and bad food, good and bad wine, are on the way out and perhaps it is a good thing. If the young generation don't appreciate the value of the good things in life as you and I know them, they not only deserve what they get, but also, of course, they don't know what they are missing.'

Not bothering to pay attention to what he was saying, Helga regarded this man. She let him talk, and he could talk! she thought. His voice had a lulling effect on her.

He talked for about ten minutes non-stop, then said abruptly, 'But I am boring you.'

Helga shook her head.

'Not at all. What you say is most interesting.'

He smiled at her. What a man! she thought.

'You may have a date, but if you haven't, suppose we lunch together? There is an excellent little restaurant not far from here.'

She thought: here is a real fast worker, but she was flattered. He must be several years younger than she was, and he kept looking at her with open admiration. Why not?

'That would be nice. First, we should introduce ourselves. I am Helga Rolfe.' She looked sharply at him to see if there was any reaction. More often than not when she mentioned her name she got a double-take, but not this time.

'Christopher Grenville.' Grenville signalled to the waiter and paid for his coffee and Helga's martini. 'Please wait a moment. I'll get my car.'

She watched him walk away: tall, beautifully-built, immaculate. She drew in a quick breath. She had made so many mistakes in the past when she had picked up men. She thought of the boy she had befriended in Bonn who had turned out to be a homo. She thought of the half-caste boy in Nassau who had turned out to be a witch doctor of all things! She thought of that wonderful-looking hunk of beef who turned out to be a blackmailing detective.* And many other mistakes, but this time, maybe she was going to be lucky.

She saw him waving to her as he forced his way against the traffic in a sleek, dark-blue Maserati. She jumped to her feet and ran across the sidewalk as he held open the off-side

* See *The Joker in the Pack*.

door for her. Horns blew, drivers shouted, but Grenville ignored them.

'Parisians have the worst driving manners except, of course, the Belgians,' he said and sent the car forward.

'Driving in Paris is a nightmare to me,' Helga said.

'Beautiful women should never drive in Paris,' Grenville said. 'They should always have an escort.'

She warmed to him.

At the end of avenue Champs-Elysées, Grenville crossed to the Left Bank. The traffic was heavy, but he handled the powerful car with expert ease. Helga was thrilled with the car.

'A Maserati?' she asked. 'I've never driven in one before.'

Grenville, thinking of what it was going to cost Patterson to hire this car, smiled.

'It's wonderful on the open road, but town work . . .'

In a few minutes, he turned off Bvd Saint Germain into a tiny side street.

'Now the problem of parking,' he said. 'Parking is a matter of patience.'

He drove around the block, then as he re-entered the narrow street, a car pulled out and Grenville, with cars behind him hooting, manoeuvred the big car into the vacant space. He was out of the car and had the off-side door open before Helga could do it herself.

'That was well done,' she said.

'When one lives in cities, one has to do this kind of thing or cease to exist.' Grenville took her arm. 'Just a short walk. You'll be amused. I hope you are hungry.'

Helga, used to the de luxe restaurants of Paris, wasn't sure that she was going to be amused when she saw the dowdy entrance of this bistro with dirty curtains, dull brass work on the door, and when Grenville opened the door, to find a long narrow room crowded with heavy, ageing Frenchmen, eating ferociously.

An enormous man, bald, with a belly like a beer barrel, came from behind the bar, his fat face, with many chins, wreathed in smiles.

'Monsieur Grenville! Impossible! How long it has been!'
And he grasped Grenville's hand, pumping it up and down.

'Claude!' Grenville said, smiling. 'I have brought a very
special friend ... Madame Rolfe.' He turned to Helga, 'This
is Claude who once was the head chef at le Tour d'Argent.
He and I have known each other for years.'

A little dazed, Helga shook hands with the enormous man
as Grenville went on, 'Something special, Claude. Nothing
too heavy. You understand?'

'Of course, Monsieur Grenville. Come this way,' and
under the staring eyes of the eaters, Claude, panting a little,
led Helga and Grenville through a doorway to a small
dining-room with four tables, comfortable, intimate and immaculate.

'But this is nice,' Helga exclaimed, surprised as Grenville
pulled out a chair for her. 'I didn't know such places existed
in Paris.'

Grenville and Claude exchanged smiles.

'They do, and this is one of my favourites,' Grenville
said as he sat down. 'Now tell me, would you like a fish
lunch?'

'Yes.'

Grenville turned to Claude.

'Then six Belons each and the *sole cardinal*. Let us have a
Muscadet.'

'Certainly, Monsieur Grenville. Perhaps an aperitif?'

Grenville looked at Helga who shook her head.

'In a few minutes, Monsieur Grenville.' Claude went
away.

'You won't be disappointed. The *sole cardinal* is the best
in Paris. The sauce is made with double cream and Danish
shrimps and lobster shells ground minutely.' He offered her
his cigarette case.

As Helga took a cigarette, she said, 'This is a beautiful
case.'

'Yes ... a present from an Austrian count. I did him a
minor service.' Grenville thought of the dreadful hours he
had spent, pushing the fat woman around the ballroom.

Helga looked sharply at him. Was there a mocking expression in the dark brown eyes?

'And what are you doing in Paris?' she asked.

'Business and pleasure.' He waved his hand in dismissal. 'I take it you are here to buy clothes. Will you be staying long?'

'I am also here on business, but I shall also be buying clothes.'

Grenville appeared to be surprised.

'I can't believe a woman as beautiful as you, can be in Paris on business. Surely not!' Then he clapped his hand to his forehead. 'Rolfe? Of course! *The* Madame Rolfe! How stupid can I be!'

The oysters arrived in a bed of crushed ice and Claude hovered.

'They are truly splendid, Monsieur Grenville. I have fed them myself.'

They were splendid.

Grenville nodded his approval, and Claude went back to the kitchen.

Smiling, Grenville said, 'So you are the fabulous Madame Rolfe. I can't pick up a newspaper without reading about you. I am flattered. And you are staying at the same hotel as I am ... what a coincidence!'

Helga looked straight at him.

'I happen to be an extremely wealthy woman who finds life often excessively boring, being in my position,' she said quietly.

Grenville regarded her, then nodded sympathetically.

'Yes. I can imagine: the prying eyes of the press, no real freedom, gossip and great responsibility.' He shook his head as he speared an oyster. 'Yes, I understand.'

'What is your business?' Helga asked abruptly. She now wanted information about this exciting man.

'This and that. Don't let us spoil a meal with sordid things like business. You have Paris at your feet, and Paris is one of the most exciting cities in the world.' Grenville then moved into one of his monologues about Paris that was so enchanting, Helga listened, spellbound. He was still talking as the

34

sole cardinal was served and he was still talking without a moment of dullness when coffee was served.

'I haven't enjoyed a meal so much nor have been so educated in years,' Helga said, smiling at him.

Grenville returned her smile, shrugging.

'Yes, the meal was good. I talk.' He shook his head. 'It is when I have a perfect companion that I talk too much. Now, alas, I have to return to business. I have a dreary appointment. Let me drive you back to the hotel.'

He left her for a few moments while he settled the check and had a word with Claude. After hand-shaking and smiles, they left the bistro and got in the Maserati.

As he started the engine, he said, 'I wonder if you would feel like repeating this. I'll try not to talk so much.' He gave her his flashing smile. 'There is a little restaurant at Fontainebleau. Would it amuse you to dine with me tomorrow night?'

Helga didn't hesitate. This man really intrigued her.

'That would be wonderful.'

He drove her back to the Plaza Athénée Hotel and escorted her to the elevator. As they waited for the cage to descend, they regarded each other.

'May I call you Helga? . . . It's a beautiful name,' Grenville said.

'Of course, Chris.'

'Then tomorrow night at eight here in the lobby?'

She nodded, touched his wrist and entered the elevator.

Joe Patterson, sitting in one of the alcoves, watched with astonishment. When Helga was whisked out of sight, Grenville strolled over to Patterson.

'There is no problem, Mr. Patterson . . . just a few more days,' then leaving Patterson gaping, he walked over to the concierge's desk.

'A card and an envelope, please,' he said.

'Certainly, monsieur.'

Grenville wrote on the card: *Thank you for your beauty, and your company. Chris.*

He put the card in the envelope, sealed it and put Helga's name on the envelope.

35

'Send twelve red roses to Madame Rolfe and charge me,' he said, then leaving the hotel, he walked to where he had parked the Maserati.

That evening, Archer and Grenville met Patterson in the grillroom of George V Hotel. Patterson was in a good mood and slightly drunk.

'You've picked the right man, Archer,' he said, after they had ordered. He grinned at Grenville. 'You're a real fast operator. You really turned the doll on. She was all over you.'

Grenville raised his eyebrows.

'It is my profession, Mr. Patterson.'

'Yeah. Well, you're a slick operator.'

They waited until the smoked salmon was served, then Patterson went on, 'I want you to understand this project, Grenville. It can't miss,' and he went on to explain about the siting of the holiday camps. Grenville listened politely while Archer, who had heard it all before, attacked his food. 'Land isn't easy to come by these days,' Patterson waved his fork, 'but I've got an option on a slice of land down in the South of France: a very fine position. I reckon I could get it and put a de luxe camp on it for around two million bucks. Your job now is to convince her to put up the money. I've got all the papers here and a beautiful brochure for her to see. You study them, and if there is anything you're not sure about, talk to Archer. He knows.'

Grenville said he would do that.

'Once you've got her on the hook,' Patterson went on, 'there are other sites. I've got my eyes on a beauty in Corsica. You could mention that to her.'

Archer decided it was time to bring Patterson down to earth.

'I must remind you, Mr. Patterson, that Helga is a tough business woman. She won't be content to act as a sleeping partner if she does put money into this project. She is likely to want part control.'

Patterson scowled.

'I won't have some goddamn woman messing around with my project.' He looked at Grenville. 'Tell her she'll get twenty-five per cent on her money, but no control!'

Rather to Archer's surprise, Grenville said smoothly, 'There should be no problem. I have every confidence I can arrange this to your satisfaction.'

Beaming, Patterson patted his arm.

'That's talking. You study all this stuff, and get it set up. How long do you reckon it'll take to get her money?'

Grenville shrugged.

There was a pause while the steaks were served, then he said, 'Most unwise to rush it, Mr. Patterson. I would say at least ten days.' He gave his flashing smile. 'I have still to get her to bed.'

'Yeah. Well, that's okay, but I want you to keep the cost down.'

'One shouldn't cut corners when going after two million dollars,' Grenville said as he cut into his steak. 'Madame Rolfe has the impression that I am wealthy. I must keep up appearances.'

'Sure, but watch it, I'm not made of money.'

'Who is these days?' Grenville said airily, and then launched into one of his monologues concerning the night life of Paris. He was so well-informed that Patterson became interested.

The meal over, Patterson asked Grenville to write down the address of a high-class brothel he had mentioned.

'I guess I'll take a look,' Patterson said and winked. He called for the check.

'Ask for Claudette,' Grenville said gravely. 'She has just that little extra.'

'Claudette, huh? Well, fine. Okay, you two. Keep in touch. Go easy on the spending,' and slightly unsteady, Patterson left the grillroom.

'What a ghastly little man,' Grenville said and waved to a waiter. 'Some brandy and more coffee, please.'

'Ghastly, yes,' Archer said, 'but he provides me with a living for the moment.'

37

'You don't believe for one moment that Helga would fall for this ridiculous project?' Grenville asked, lifting his eyebrows.

Archer shook his head.

'Of course not, but as long as Patterson thinks she will, then I get a hundred dollars a week and you get fun and luxury.'

'And when she turns it down? What then?'

Archer lifted his heavy shoulders.

'Then I suppose you look for a rich old woman to fleece, and I look for yet another promoter.'

Grenville dropped sugar into his coffee.

'You are not serious, are you?'

Archer looked sharply at him.

'One must face facts.'

'My dear Jack, surely that is being defeatist. Let us look at this situation. In a few hours, I have captivated one of the richest women in the world. She is longing to drag me into her bed. Once we become lovers – and that will be soon – worked carefully, thought out carefully, I shall have access to her millions. I have to admit plotting and planning has never been my forte. I was under the impression it was your department. Correct me if I am wrong, and then there is nothing more to be said.'

'Go on,' Archer said, now very alert. 'You have more to say.'

'I suggest we drop Patterson, and you and I work together, and get as much money as we can from Helga.'

Archer considered this for a long moment, then shook his head.

'Not good thinking, Chris. Without Patterson's financial backing, neither you nor I will get very far. You won't be driving around in a Maserati or staying at the Plaza Athénée, and I shall be in financial trouble. I agree it would be an excellent idea to get rid of Patterson, but what do we do for money? And another thing, so far you have only seen the best side of Helga. I know her. Her other side is toughness, shrewdness and an excellent financial brain. Let me tell you something about her. She was the daughter of a brilliant international lawyer, and she has impressive degrees in law and economics. She worked with her father in Lausanne where I was a partner so I know her capabilities. Don't ever take her lightly. She is very quick to smell a con. I would say she is mentally as brilliant as the best, and that is saying a lot. Her weakness, of course, is sex, but I believe that sex would take second place if she suspected she was being taken for a ride.'

'That remains to be seen,' Grenville said. 'I am glad to have the information, but I still think we can drop Patterson – not immediately, of course – and make a killing with Helga. This now depends on you, Jack. Surely, with your brains, you can think up some scheme where we can pick up a couple of million off her. I assure you I'll handle Helga, providing you can think of a bright idea.'

Archer half-closed his eyes while he thought. Helga had bested him in the last battle and had treated him abominably. It would be nice to get his revenge, but how?

'I'll have to think about it,' he said.

'That's what I am suggesting. We have ten days. We can still get this horrible little man to finance us. We can encourage him to think all is going well, then we drop him. So think about it.'

'Again I must warn you, Chris, not to take Helga lightly,' Archer said. 'She can be very tricky.'

Grenville gave his musical laugh.

'If you had seen the way she looked at me this afternoon, you wouldn't worry. She is ripe for picking.'

Back in his sleazy hotel bedroom, Archer stretched out on his bed. His active, shrewd mind remained busy for the next two hours, but no plan to get two million dollars from Helga presented itself.

Frustrated, and now tired, he turned on his small radio for the 23.00 news. The big story was the holding of five hostages at Orly airport with a ransom demand of ten million francs.

Impatiently, Archer snapped off the radio, then getting

off the bed, he began to undress. Then suddenly, half-way out of his shirt, he paused and looked at the radio, standing on the bedside table.

Was this the germ of an idea? he asked himself.

He scarcely slept that night.

Relais de Flore is a tiny restaurant in a back street near the Fontainebleau palais. Helga and Grenville were welcomed by the proprietress, Madame Tonnelle, who led them into the small restaurant with only fifteen tables.

As Helga settled in her chair, Grenville said, 'I have already ordered. I want you to experience one of the great dishes of France: *chicken Oliver*. It is quite remarkable, and Madame Tonnelle has learned to cook it. I suggest we have a *fond d'artichaut* in vinaigrette while we wait.'

Helga, looking splendid in an apricot-coloured trouser suit, smiled at him.

'You seem to know so much about Paris, Chris. This place is just what I like. I get so bored with the de. luxe restaurants.'

She was thinking: 'I've never met such an intriguing man! He must be marvellous in bed! He could be marvellous as a husband!'

'I get around,' Grenville said, shrugging. 'I would love to take you to restaurants in Vienna, in Prague, in Moscow. Now let me tell you about the *chicken Oliver*. First, Oliver is one of the great creators of dishes in France. The preparation of the chicken is too complicated to go into now. The ingredients are many: six yolks of egg, thick cream, butter, cognac, tarragon, shallots, celery hearts and so on. The exciting thing is that finally a lobster sauce is poured over the chicken.'

'It sounds out of this world,' Helga said, impressed.

'It is exceptional.' Grenville smiled at her. 'For an exceptionally beautiful woman.'

Again Helga warmed to him.

While they were eating the *fond d'artichaut*, she said, 'Chris, tell me what do you do for a living?'

Grenville had had a call from Archer that morning who had asked him to meet him at a bistro off Rue de Sèvres.

Archer had said, 'I have a germ of an idea, but I need to work on it. Now, here is what you do,' and he went on to explain in detail how Grenville should handle Helga. Grenville, listening intently, kept nodding.

'Take her out tonight and leave her at the hotel. Don't go to bed with her,' Archer said, 'I know Helga: the longer she is kept waiting, the easier she is to handle. Then tomorrow, leave the hotel for two days. Send her a nice message saying you are called away on business. Let her stew, and she will. Then after two days, return to the hotel and put her to bed. By then, I think, you should have no trouble with her.'

Grenville accepted this advice.

In answer to Helga's question, he shrugged. 'I have a private income from the Grenville trust that takes care of my day-to-day expenses. At the moment, I am working for a rich American who is promoting a property scheme. I have to meet dreary business men and try to interest them to put up the necessary money.' He smiled. 'It passes the time, and who knows? I could find someone, and then I will get an acceptable rake-off.'

'What is the scheme?' Helga asked.

'Nothing that could possibly interest you,' Grenville said, acting on Archer's coaching. 'Anyway, who wants to talk business when I have a lovely woman as a companion?'

At this moment Madame Tonnelle arrived with the chicken. It was the most delicious meal Helga could remember eating.

While they ate, Helga let Grenville talk, but she only half-listened. She was thinking about what he had said. A property scheme? She had so much money! Perhaps she could get involved in this scheme and then get a hold on this intriguing man.

It wasn't until they were in the Maserati, driving back to Paris, that she said, 'This property scheme, Chris. Is it something I could be interested in?'

Grenville smiled to himself. How well Archer knew this woman!

'Decidedly not. You have all your time taken up with the Rolfe Electronics. No . . . definitely not for you.'

'But how do you know?' Helga said sharply. 'It could interest me!'

'I couldn't discuss it with you without my boss's say-so. Sorry, Helga, but that's how it is, and I do assure you, you wouldn't be interested.'

'Very well,' Helga said, frowning.

Grenville then began to tell her the history of the Fontaine-bleau forest, but she paid little attention. She was curious about this property scheme and felt frustrated, as Archer had assured Grenville she would be. If this scheme was interesting, she thought, it could give her a new outlet for her money, and it could also, much, much more important, give her Chris.

They arrived back at the Plaza Athénée Hotel.

'Unhappily, I now have a business date with my boss,' Grenville said as they entered the lobby. 'It has been a wonderful evening, and thank you for your company.'

Watched by Patterson, who was sitting in one of the alcoves, Helga looked at Grenville.

'And thank you,' she said. 'It really has been fabulous. That chicken!'

Grenville escorted her to the elevator, kissed her hand, looked at her for a long moment, and then left her.

In her suite, and although it was only 23.00, Helga undressed and dropped into bed.

She felt relaxed and happy.

She was in love with this man. That look he had given her as they had parted at the elevator told her he too was in love with her. No man, she told herself, could look like that without being in love, but then she didn't know just how professional Grenville was.

Lying in bed, she had a moment of panic, realizing that Grenville had said nothing about meeting her the following day. The thought of being in Paris without him depressed her. Paris would be nothing without him! Relax, she told herself. He is in love with me. Tomorrow, he will telephone, and we will go somewhere marvellous together, but she couldn't drift off into sleep, and finally, she once again took two sleeping pills.

She slept late. Awakening after ten o'clock, she ordered coffee, then took a bath. As she was dressing, the telephone bell rang. Eagerly, she snatched up the receiver.

'The desk, madame,' an obsequious voice said. 'There is a message for you. Shall I send it up?'

Disappointed that it wasn't Grenville, Helga snapped, 'Yes,' and hung up.

A few minutes later a page arrived with a bunch of roses and an envelope.

The message sent her into the depths of despair.

I am called away on dreary business. I loved our evening together. May I hope, in two days' time, we can meet again? Chris.

Two days!

But there was hope! He wanted to see her again! She must wait!

Going to the window, she looked down at the traffic moving in the bright sunshine. There would be no spring for her for the next two days.

And the next two days were purgatory for her as Archer had intended them to be. Loman suggested she should go with him and Winborn to Versailles where there was a possible site for the new factory. She went with them because she had nothing better to do. They spent the day discussing the site with a minor minister. Helga couldn't work up any enthusiasm. Her mind was continually on Grenville. The minor minister invited them to dinner to finalize the plan, and again, because she couldn't bear the thought of being on her own, Helga joined them in the Plaza Athénée grillroom.

The following day, she, Loman and Winborn had lunch with the French Prime Minister. Again, she was utterly bored, wondering what Grenville was doing, and if he was thinking of her as she was continually thinking of him. She had a lonely dinner in her suite and two sleeping pills, with the thought that tomorrow, she would see him again.

Grenville had driven out of Paris and had had two enjoyable days at the Host du Château, Fere-en-Tardenois where he ate well and toured the Marne 1914–18 battlefields. He liked being on his own, spending Patterson's money and he didn't give Helga even a thought.

He arrived back at the Plaza Athénée Hotel around 11.00, two days after his departure. He called Archer from his suite.

'Go in and win,' Archer said. 'I've talked to Patterson. He is getting restive,' and he went on to tell Grenville exactly how he should handle Helga.

Grenville said he would follow Archer's suggestions, then added, 'The trouble now, Jack, is I'm running out of money.'

'That is something you must talk to Patterson about,' Archer said. 'There's nothing I can do about that.'

So Grenville went to Patterson's room. He found him and Shappilo studying a large-scale map of Corsica.

'What's going on?' Patterson demanded aggressively. 'Where the hell have you been these past two days?'

Grenville took a chair and smiled at Patterson.

'I have been keeping a pair of pants hot,' he said. 'Jack and I discussed the situation. He agreed I should go off for two days and let the lady simmer. It'll pay off tonight.'

Shappilo said, 'That's good thinking, Mr. Patterson.'

Patterson grunted.

'So what's going to happen tonight?'

'I will explain the Blue Sky thing to her and then put her to bed.'

Patterson thought, then nodded.

'Sounds okay, and then what?'

Grenville lifted his hands.

'That depends. I think she will go along with the idea, but one never knows. It is the beginning of the operation. She might bite at once. If not, then I will continue to work on her, but I assure you, Mr. Patterson, in at least ten days, you will get the money.'

'Well, okay.' Patterson pulled at his cigar and released a cloud of smoke. 'It's your baby . . . you handle it.'

'Which I will do, but it is now a matter of more money, Mr. Patterson,' Grenville said smoothly. 'Your five thousand francs has run away. If you want me to continue this operation, I need another five thousand francs.'

Patterson glared at him.

'You don't get another dime out of me, Grenville! You finance yourself! When this deal jells you'll get a cut, but from now on, you finance yourself!'

'Unfortunately, Mr. Patterson,' Grenville said, 'I have no finances. I thought that was understood. You either give me five thousand francs or the operation is off . . . it is as simple as that.'

Patterson's face turned purple.

'What have you done with the money I have given you?' he barked. 'I want an accounting!'

'That I can give you,' Grenville got to his feet. 'Frankly, Mr. Patterson, when two million dollars are involved, I find your attitude extraordinary. Well, shall we forget the whole thing? I have other irons in the fire, and this haggling over money bores me.'

Patterson hesitated, looked at Shappilo who nodded, then he took out his wallet. He counted out three one thousand franc notes and put them on the table.

'That's all you're going to get!'

Grenville shook his head, his expression sad.

'Such a pity. All right, Mr. Patterson, then let us forget it all. You could, of course, find someone else. I said five thousand francs, and I mean five thousand francs.' He turned and smiled at Shappilo. 'I shall be leaving this afternoon. I have an interesting proposition in Madrid: a very wealthy widow who wants to buy a castle.' He shrugged. 'Poor Helga Rolfe! But for a tiny sum of two thousand francs, she is going to lose a lover, but I always say one woman's loss is another woman's gain.' As he moved to the door, he waved to Patterson. 'Bye, Mr. Patterson.'

'Hey, wait!'

Grenville paused and lifted his eyebrows.

'Here's your goddamn five thousand! But you deliver . . .!'

As Patterson added two more one thousand francs to the money on the table, Grenville walked back, picked up the money and stared at Patterson.

'I think I mentioned this before, Mr. Patterson: never threaten me. It is my habit to deliver,' and using this as his exit line, he left the suite.

CHAPTER THREE

A LITTLE after 09.00, a waiter brought Helga her breakfast, and on the tray was a sealed envelope. Scarcely waiting for the waiter to leave, she tore open the envelope to find the following message:

Unless I hear from you, may I knock on your door at 20.30? I have missed your beauty and your company. Chris.

Helga was ecstatic. As she drank her coffee, her mind became busy.

Tonight! she thought.

This time she would take control. No more driving to some little bistro. They would eat here in her suite and then . . . !

She had the whole day to make preparations. A splendid dinner served in her suite, no waiters, to hell with gossip, then Chris in her bed!

The telephone bell rang. It was Winborn, saying he and Loman were going to Versailles again. When would she be ready to go with them?

Who cared about a site in Versailles? This was Paris in the spring!

'I have a headache. You and Fred handle it,' she said curtly and hung up.

She called the Plaza Athénée hairdresser and told him to come at 15.00.

'I want your beautician too,' she said.

'Certainly, Madame Rolfe.'

She took a bath, and as she lay in the scented water, she

kept thinking of Grenville. Tonight! She closed her eyes, imagining him taking her gently, his lips against hers and she released a little moan of ecstasy.

Later, dressed in a pale-blue trouser suit, she telephoned the concierge and asked for the maitre d'hôtel to come up.

When he arrived, she said, 'I want dinner here for two. This must be something special. What do you suggest?'

'It depends on your taste, madame,' the maitre d'hôtel returned. 'Would you give me an indication: fish, meat, poultry?'

'I want something special,' Helga repeated impatiently. 'I don't want waiters here. I want a serve-it-yourself dinner, but it must be impeccable.'

'Certainly, madame. Then I suggest lobster mousse and *noisette de veau au morilles*, cheese naturally, and perhaps a champagne sorbet. The *noisette de veau* is one of our specialities and can be left on a hot plate. There will be no need for a waiter, madame.'

Helga nodded.

'If that is the best you can suggest . . .'

'I assure you, madame, you will not be disappointed. Champagne, and no other wines.'

'Then at eight o'clock.'

'It will be arranged, madame.'

At a bistro on the Left Bank, Archer and Grenville conferred.

'This is D-day,' Grenville said. 'I take her to bed tonight. I managed to squeeze another five thousand out of that horrible little man. You had better have a cut,' and he offered Archer a thousand franc note.

Archer, who was getting worried by the way his money was disappearing in expensive Paris, eagerly took the money.

'I've read through all this junk Patterson gave me,' Grenville went on. 'Surely no one in their right mind would invest money in such a scheme?'

'It is possible, but extremely unlikely,' Archer said. 'It is a gamble, but I am quite sure Helga won't be interested. She is far too shrewd to put her money in such a project. Now, here is what you tell her ...'

For the next half hour, Grenville listened, then finally, when Archer had finished his coaching, Grenville nodded.

'Yes. I go along with all that, but after ...? When she turns me down? What do we do? Have you thought up an idea, Jack?'

'I have the germ of an idea, but it is too early yet to discuss it. Get her to bed. This is the important thing. Once in bed, she is yours.' Archer smiled. 'And mine.'

At 20.00, two waiters arrived at Helga's suite and set up a table, placed a hot plate on a trolley and two ice buckets, containing bottles of champagne. While they worked, Helga, burning with impatience, kept looking at her watch. She had on a Dior fine wool suit in apricot. Her jewellery was simple: gold ear-rings and gold bracelets. She was looking her magnificent best.

The maitre d'hôtel arrived and supervised the final touches to the table.

'All is now ready, madame,' he said. 'Nothing will spoil. I am sure you will be satisfied.'

Helga nodded.

'Thank you.' She gave him a hundred fanc note, and he left, bowing.

She paced around the suite, continually looking at her watch. As the minute hand moved to 20.30, there came a tap on the door. She had to restrain herself from running. She opened the door.

Grenville, in a dark immaculately cut suit, wearing the Old Etonian tie, took her hand and brushed it with his lips.

'How beautiful you look!' he exclaimed. 'It seems a century since I last saw you.' As he entered the suite, he saw the laid table. 'But Helga! I was going to take you ...'

'Not tonight,' she said, a little breathlessly. 'This is my turn. Let's have a drink.' She waved to the bottles on a separate table. 'I'll have a vodka martini.'

'My drink too,' Grenville said, and putting a brief-case he was carrying on a chair, he began to mix the drink. 'Have you been shopping?' He smiled at her. 'Buying up Balmain?'

'No. I've been walking over a dreary building site with two very dreary colleagues. And you?'

Grenville laughed.

'I was doing exactly the same.' He carried the drinks to a table, and as Helga sat down, he pulled up a chair near her. 'What are we going to eat?'

She sipped her drink and nodded her approval.

'This is as good as Hinkle makes.'

'Hinkle?'

'My old and faithful major-domo whom I have left in my Florida home. He makes the most divine omelettes.'

Grenville wasn't interested in old and faithful major-domos.

'But you haven't told me what we are going to eat?'

'You sound hungry.'

He gave her his flashing smile.

'I am. I am only just back from Nice. I couldn't face that awful stuff they serve on the plane, so I haven't eaten all day.'

He had, in fact, paused on the way back to Paris in the Maserati to have a light lunch, but Grenville could never resist gaining sympathy from women.

'Nice? I love the south of France. Drink up then, and let's eat.'

While Grenville served the lobster mousse, Helga kept looking at him. She kept thinking: he really is marvellous! There is that wonderful thing about him no other man I've ever known has had.

'Tell me about Nice,' she said, as they began to eat.

'Actually, Helga, I want your advice. I may have to go to Saudi Arabia in a couple of days' time and, frankly, I don't want to go.'

This was a shock to Helga. She looked at him, stiffening.

'Saudi Arabia? But why?'

She thought 'Dear God! Am I going to lose him?'

'It is rather a long story, but if you can bear with it, I'll tell you.' He took another helping of the mousse. 'This is quite excellent. Won't you have more?'

Helga shook her head.

'Tell me about Saudi Arabia.'

'It's this stupid project,' Grenville said. 'For you to understand, let me lightly sketch in the background. I have an income from England, left me by my father (a lie). At one time, it was acceptable, but no longer. When the pound sterling was strong, I was very comfortably off, but now, with the present currency exchange, I am, frankly, having a struggle to live the way I wish to live, so I have accepted this stupid job which was offered me by an American property promoter. He is the world's worst bore. He has a pipe dream of promoting holiday camps in the sunspots of Europe. He wants money. He decided I could raise the money. I've talked to a number of wealthy business men, but they aren't interested. Now he imagines there is so much money in Saudi Arabia they will fall over themselves to give him the money. I am sure this is sheer nonsense, but he wants me to go. He offers to pay my expenses, and also, quite a handsome retainer.' He pushed his plate aside, then shrugged. 'I think I'll have to go.'

Getting up, he took away their plates and served the *noisette de veau.*

'This looks marvellous,' he said, as he carried the plates to the table. 'I love this serve-yourself idea of yours.'

But Helga's mind was busy. She had only five more days in France, then she would be returning to Paradise City. She couldn't bear the thought of Grenville going off to Saudi Arabia and leaving her on her own.

She forced a smile.

'I thought it would please you. Tell me about this project, Chris.'

She's biting, he thought, but waved his hand deprecatingly.

'It just wouldn't be interesting to you or to anyone,' he said as he began to eat. 'Hmm . . . this is really good!'

'I want to know about it!' The sudden snap in her voice startled him.

'All right, but later. Actually, I have all the papers here.'

He nodded to the brief-case, lying on the chair, and that was his false move.

Archer had warned him to be very careful how he handled Helga, but seeing her determined interest, he had allowed himself to be just too confident.

Seeing his confident smile, Helga regarded him. A red light flashed up in her mind. Archer had told Grenville that she was shrewd and quick to smell a con and he knew Helga: this warning was meant to be taken seriously, but Grenville, so used to dealing with rich, stupid women, hadn't taken the warning seriously enough.

Helga was now asking herself if this was an opening gambit for some swindle. Now, looking at Grenville, who was happily eating, she told herself not to be so suspicious, but the red light was up. She wanted this man. She wanted him in her bed. But suppose this was a set-up?

Probing, she said casually, 'Is this site in Nice?'

'No. It is in Vallauris. It is quite an impressive piece of land with marvellous views.'

'How many hectares?'

Grenville had no idea. He shrugged.

'It's all in the plan, but let's enjoy this, Helga. I had no idea they could cook so well here. Wouldn't you like a little more?' He poured more champagne.

'No more for me, thank you.'

He was aware that she was studying him, her blue eyes uncomfortably direct.

'Don't look so serious, Helga,' he said. 'I've told you this project couldn't possibly interest you, and I am also certain that the new Arabian king wouldn't part with a dollar.'

'Who is this American you are working for? What is his name?'

Grenville hesitated.

'His name? Joe Patterson. Actually, he is staying in this hotel.'

'Short, fat and pock-marked?'

Grenville almost gaped at her.

'That's right, and the world's worst bore.'

'I have seen him. How much does he want to promote this holiday camp?'

Grenville had an uneasy feeling that the initiative was slipping away from him. This woman, looking directly at him, began to worry him.

'Two million dollars.' He laughed. 'According to him, that takes care of buying the site and putting up the camp, but who in their right mind, these days, would put up two million?' He grimaced. 'Not that it wouldn't be a marvellous deal for me. I get a two per cent cut, and that would be nice money.'

Again the red light flashed up in Helga's mind.

'Yes, I can understand why you are interested, Chris.' She sipped her champagne.

'Well, I'm sure it won't come off, but it might be amusing to go to Saudi Arabia. I've never been there.'

'Have you any introductions?' The probing note in her voice again worried Grenville.

'I believe Mr. Patterson is arranging that.'

Helga nodded, then laid down her knife and fork.

'Do help yourself, Chris. I'm sure you must still be starving.'

'Well, it's so good ...'

While he was helping himself at the trolley, Helga lit a cigarette.

'A holiday camp?' she said. 'That might not be a bad investment. Two million? Vallauris? What would Mr. Patterson's terms be if someone advanced the money?'

Grenville stared, then returned to the table, his plate loaded, and sat down.

'He is offering twenty-five per cent on the money.'

'That seems excessively generous. The banks would accept a lot less.'

Grenville shrugged. He wished she would stop talking. He was thoroughly enjoying the meal.

'I wouldn't know about that, Helga.'

'And how about control?'

'From what I understand, he wants to keep control, but

why bother? Surely you wouldn't be remotely interested?'

There was a long pause which made him uneasy. As he ate, he looked from time to time at her. She sat still, her blue eyes cloudy, her face expressionless.

'Look, Helga . . .'

She lifted her hand in an impatient gesture.

'Enjoy it, Chris . . . I'm thinking,' and the steely note in her voice made Grenville suddenly lose his appetite. He pushed aside his plate.

'I've had more than enough.'

'There is cheese and a sorbet,' Helga said. 'Do help yourself.'

'What about you?'

'Coffee, please.'

He got up, reluctantly deciding to pass up the cheese, and poured two cups of coffee and sat at the table again. He could sense a change had come over her, but he couldn't define the change. She now seemed remote and her expression had hardened.

'Let me see these papers, Chris.'

Some forty minutes ago, her body had been yearning to be taken. All day long, she had thought of this man, but now, with a growing conviction that she was being set up for a con, her desire for him faded.

As Archer, who knew her so well, had warned Grenville: 'I believe that sex would take second place, if she suspected she was being taken for a ride.'

Sex was now taking second place.

'Are you sure you want to be bothered?' Grenville had an uneasy feeling that she was beginning to dominate him, and this worried him. Always, he had been able to control the women who had fallen for him.

'I asked you to show me these papers, Chris!' There was sudden steel in her voice.

A little flustered, and losing his cool, Grenville opened the brief-case and took out the coloured brochure and the plan of the site.

'Give yourself a brandy . . . nothing for me,' Helga said,

and sitting back, studied the brochure, then the plan of the site, while Grenville, sure now he had lost control of the situation, wandered to the drinks table and poured himself a brandy.

'You will see ...' he began, but she silenced him with an impatient wave of her hand.

'Let me read this first!'

He cut himself a piece of cheese and ate it. Holding his brandy glass, he wandered over to the window, drew aside the drapes and stared down at the traffic. This woman, he warned himself, was going to be difficult, but he thought of the possibilities. Although his confidence in himself had been shaken, he was still sure, that once he could get her to bed, all would go well.

Finally, she put down the papers. Her sharp mind had absorbed the details. She realized this promotion would never get off the ground, but she did see how she could control this man who meant so much to her. It was ridiculously easy.

'This could be interesting,' she said. 'Let us talk about it.' She moved to the settee, and Grenville came over, and sat by her side. 'I have so much money and I believe money should always be put to work. If Mr. Patterson is really prepared to pay twenty-five per cent on two million ... yes, it is interesting.'

Grenville stared at her.

'But, Helga, dear! Surely you ...?'

She waved him to silence.

'Two million is nothing to me, and it would be nice for you to get two per cent. Now, this is what we will do. You and I will look at this site at Vallauris. I love the south of France. It'll be fun, and also business. We will stay at Cannes for a couple of days. The Carlton Hotel is always so kind to me. Don't worry about expenses: leave all that to me. Tell your Mr. Patterson that I am interested, and that you have persuaded me to look at the site. Telling him that will ensure, if the deal goes through, that you will get your commission.' She patted his hand. 'Let us catch the 22.30 night flight tomorrow. What do you think?'

Dazed, Grenville nodded.

'That would be wonderful. I'll tell Mr. Patterson. He will be delighted.'

'I am sure he will.' The blue eyes were steely. 'All right, Chris, this has been very exciting. I have had a long day. Leave all the arrangements to me. Let us meet in the lobby tomorrow evening at 19.00. Then together, we will fly to Nice.'

He realized, with a sense of shock, that she was dismissing him.

'I was hoping . . .' he began, but stopped as she got to her feet.

'Later, Chris . . . then tomorrow.'

As he reached for the papers and the brochure, she said curtly, 'Leave those. I want to study them. Good night, Chris. I am sure we are going to have fun.'

For the first time in his career as a gigolo, Grenville felt completely dominated. He kissed her hand, then bewildered, he let himself out of the suite. He stood in the corridor for several moments, then pulling himself together, he hurried to his own suite. He telephoned Archer and gave him a blow-by-blow account of the evening.

He heard Archer draw in a deep breath of exasperation.

'I told you she was nobody's fool!' Archer exploded. 'I warned you! You've blown it! She now knows this is a con!'

'But she is taking me to Vallauris tomorrow!' Grenville said, his voice high-pitched. 'If she knows it is a con, why should she do that?'

'That shows how little you know about her, but you'll learn,' Archer said sourly. 'She is after your body. Now listen, Chris, do exactly what she wants you to do. Don't argue with her. Go along with her. My idea is germinating.'

'For God's sake! What idea?'

'Give me a few more days, and remember, Chris, don't ever imagine *you* can outsmart Helga. She is very special.' He paused, then went on, 'But *I* can. Go along with her, and leave the rest to me,' and hung up.

*

56

Grenville stood on the balcony of his room at the Carlton Hotel, Cannes, feeling the hot sun against his face. He looked down at the crowded Croisette. For the first time in his gigolo life, he felt unsure of himself and unhappy.

The previous day, in Paris, he had talked to Patterson, telling him that Helga wanted to see the site at Vallauris. Patterson beamed and clapped Grenville on his shoulder.

'So she's biting! You're doing a swell job, Grenville! When she sees the site, she's going to get really steamed up! It's a beaut! Now, here's what you do: call Henri Leger when you get to Cannes. You'll find him in the book. He's the guy who is handling the site. He'll take you both there. Once she has seen it, the deal's as good as fixed!'

Grenville had hoped to see Helga, but the concierge at the Plaza Athénée Hotel had told him that Madame Rolfe had gone out and he had no idea when she would be returning.

After a lonely, unhappy day, wandering around Paris, Grenville was in his suite when Helga telephoned. The time was 18.00.

'See you in an hour, Chris, in the lobby,' she said briskly. 'Everything is arranged. Bring enough clothes for a week.'

Never before had a woman given him orders. He attempted to assert himself.

'Helga ... I ...'

She cut him short.

'Later, Chris ... I have people here,' and she hung up.

Then Archer telephoned.

'How is it going?' he asked.

'God knows!' Grenville said. 'She's getting on top of me! I don't know if I can stand her much longer! She's treating me like a damned gigolo!'

Archer laughed sourly.

'That's what you are, aren't you? Take it easy. My brain child is getting underway. When you get to the Carlton, telephone me. Now, remember, Chris, be her gigolo ... get her into bed!'

Angrily, Grenville slammed down the receiver.

But he was in the lobby at 19.00 with a suitcase. He was

aware that Patterson, sitting in an alcove, a whisky in his hand, was watching.

Helga appeared with the manager of the hotel. There were elaborate good-byes, tips, hand-shaking while Grenville stood and watched.

Finally, Helga came to him, smiling.

'Let's go, Chris.' She laughed. He thought she was looking young and marvellous, and very alive.

There was a chauffeur-driven Cadillac waiting. While they were being driven to Orly airport, Helga chatted. She had had a dreadful day with her colleagues.

'The fuss men make about buying a site!' she exclaimed and threw up her hands. 'I'm so glad to get away from them! Tell me, Chris, what have you been doing today?'

What had he been doing? Nothing, but he pulled himself together, and launched into a fictitious visit to a picture gallery on the Left Bank, but he quickly realized she wasn't listening.

There were two porters to handle the luggage at the airport. There was an air hostess to take them to the V.I.P. lounge. Grenville was aware that he was just an onlooker, a role that irritated him, and he realized for the first time, the power of Rolfe's millions. On the plane, two air hostesses administered to them. The Flight captain came and shook hands with Helga, ignoring Grenville. She seemed to know him for she asked after his children. Grenville found he was no more than a stooge, and he turned sulky, but Helga apparently didn't notice. She talked gaily, laughed and enjoyed herself.

There was a Mercedes waiting for them at the Nice airport. The chauffeur, an elderly man, took off his cap as Helga approached. She shook hands with him, and asked after his wife, while Grenville waited, feeling like a dummy.

The drive to Cannes took only twenty minutes. The manager of the Carlton Hotel was there to greet Helga. He bowed distantly to Grenville, scarcely seeing him as Helga introduced him to Grenville.

'Chris, I'm tired . . . tomorrow,' she said, and was whisked away, while he took the second elevator to his room.

Now, this morning, a note arrived with his breakfast.

Bore! I have business. Enjoy yourself. Meet me in the lobby at 21.00. Helga.

This woman was beginning to frighten him. He had told her he had visited the site at Vallauris. Now, he realised how stupid that lie had been. She would expect him to take her there tomorrow, and he hadn't the vaguest idea where the site was! He had to do something about that! He called Henri Leger's office.

A girl said, 'Monsieur Leger is out. He won't be back until this afternoon.'

'I am acting on behalf of Mr. Joe Patterson who has an option on a site at Vallauris,' Grenville said. 'Can you tell me where the site is situated?'

'Mr. Leger is on the site now,' the girl told him. 'Madame Rolfe is with him.'

Grenville felt a chilly sensation run up his spine.

'It's all right, don't bother,' he said and hung up.

He remembered Archer's warning. *Don't ever imagine you can outsmart Helga.*

Well, all right, he thought, then I play along with her. The crunch will come after I have slept with her. That is what Archer has kept telling me. At least, I am covered. I have always told her this promotion is ridiculous.

He put a call through to Archer.

'It's all right,' Archer said, after listening to Grenville's tale. 'By now, she has found out Patterson's promotion is a lemon, but she is still interested in you. Play the innocent. I'm coming down, and I'll be at the Clarice Hotel tonight. I am almost ready with my idea. Take it easy, Chris. We are going to get two million dollars out of her. She's smart, but I am smarter.'

Grenville hoped to God he was.

He was in the lobby at 21.00, after spending a day

wandering around the shops at Cannes, then taking a swim, but not enjoying a moment of it.

Helga, in a turquoise-coloured silk chiffon dress and a white fox stole, swept out of the elevator and joined him.

'Chris! I'm starving! We are going to the Boule d'or. Did you have a lovely day?'

Without waiting for his reply, she swept through the lobby, and to where the Mercedes was waiting.

They were driven swiftly to a restaurant overlooking the harbour where Helga received a royal welcome while Grenville, feeling more and more inadequate, stood around, until the welcome was over.

'My husband and I always ate here,' Helga explained as they settled at a table on the terrace. 'Louis can be relied on.' She smiled at the maitre d'hôtel as he hurried to her side. 'Louis! So good to see you again! We want a lovely dinner. Suggest something.'

'Madame, why not your favourite: crêpes with shrimps and tuna fish, and a boned duck with prunes?'

Helga looked at Grenville.

'It is wonderful. Why not?'

Grenville hesitated. He longed to assert himself, but his confidence had gone. 'All right.'

'Now you choose the wines, Chris. You are so expert.'

That, at least, gave him back some initiative. He began to examine the wine list as the wine waiter hovered. Then just as he was about to order, Helga said, 'Jacques, have you that divine Margaux '29 which my husband so enjoyed?'

The wine waiter bowed.

'Just two bottles left, madame.'

'Oh, Chris, you must try that, and they have a wonderful Domaine de Chevalier.'

Defeated and deflated, Grenville closed the wine list.

'Anything you say, Helga.'

He now realized she was completely dominating him. A Margaux '29 would cost at least five hundred francs, but he remembered Archer's advice: play along with her!

She looked at him, her eyes sparkling.

'This is fun, Chris. Tell me about your day.'

'My day? Oh, I wandered around, had a swim, and missed you.'

That pleased her and she patted his hand.

'I missed you too, but tomorrow will be different. We can enjoy ourselves. I'm dying for a swim.'

'And what did you do?' he asked, knowing already what she had done.

'Let's talk about that later.' The direct stare made him uneasy.

So they ate the meal which was excellent, and talked about this and that. Grenville found he wasn't able to launch into one of his monologues, although he wanted to tell her about Monte Carlo and the Rainiers. Somehow, Helga dominated the conversation, telling him of her experiences when Herman Rolfe and she had spent many weeks in Cannes.

The meal finished, she said, 'Let's return to the hotel.'

To his relief, she signed the check and gave a lavish tip.

He said rather feebly, 'This should be on me, Helga,' but apparently, she didn't hear.

Driven back to the hotel, they went together to her suite. She walked out onto the balcony and looked at the sea, the crowds, the palm trees and the lights.

'I love Cannes,' she said, as Grenville joined her.

'Yes: it is special.'

He stood by her side, uneasy and worried.

'Now let's talk business.' She dropped into a chair.

Grenville wished Archer was here. This woman was demoralizing him. He had never met a woman with her strength of character; never before heard such sudden steel in her voice, or had to meet such a direct stare.

'Business? Of course.' He sat beside her. 'You mean the Patterson thing.'

She smiled at him.

'Chris, you have many splendid talents, but property promotion is not for you.'

Grenville crossed his long legs and opened his gold cigarette case, which he offered. Helga took a cigarette and he did. He lit the cigarettes before saying, 'You could be right.'

She threw back her head and laughed. Looking at her, Grenville suddenly realized she was really a beautiful woman. Her throat line was superb.

'When you told me about this Blue Sky promotion and that you had become involved,' Helga said, 'I decided to check. Yesterday, I instructed my people to investigate Joe Patterson. This morning I inspected the site at Vallauris. Now, let me tell you what I have discovered. First, Joe Patterson: he has spent five years in a U.S. jail for fraud. He has very little money: just enough to keep up appearances. The Blue Sky promotion is yet another of his many swindles. I went this morning to the cadastre at Vallauris. They told me that there are two footpaths through this piece of land, so it would be impossible to build. Leger, the agent, is a crook. You now have to face the fact, Chris, that you have got yourself involved in a swindle.'

Taking out his handkerchief, Grenville wiped his damp hands.

'I did say, didn't I, Helga, no one in their right minds . . .?'

'Yes,' she broke in. It irked him that she kept cutting him short. 'We can forget Patterson. I'm sorry, because you won't get the two per cent on this so-called deal.'

Grenville shrugged.

'Life is like that, isn't it? I never really thought I would.' He stared down at the crowd, moving on the promenade. 'Maybe I had better see this farce to the end. If Patterson really wants me to go to Saudi Arabia, it could pay me to do so.'

He thought this was a smart move, and looked at Helga. But her searching stare made him immediately uncomfortable. He forced himself to smile at her.

'Forget Saudi Arabia,' Helga said curtly. 'I have a suggestion to make.'

'You have? What is it, Helga?'

'My corporation can use your talents. I want you to become a member of my executive staff.'

With an effort, Grenville kept his face expressionless.

'But I know nothing about electronics.'

'You won't need to. I want you as my personal assistant.' Helga put her hand on his. 'You can't imagine how many things I have to deal with, and with you at my side, my work would be halved. What do you think?'

Here it is, Grenville thought and suddenly gained confidence. His fingers caressed Helga's wrist.

'I would love that, but tell me first: your personal assistant?' He looked at her with that sensual look he could produce for middle-aged or elderly women that had never failed. 'How personal?'

'Very, very personal, Chris, darling,' Helga said and got to her feet.

As he went with her into the bedroom, Grenville thought that this time he hadn't fluffed it. He could almost hear Archer applauding on the sidelines.

The warm sun, coming through the slats of the shutters, woke Helga. She moved voluptuously, sighing, then opened her eyes. Looking at the bedside clock, she saw it was 10.00.

She had never slept so well. Turning on her side, she looked at the pillow beside her and touched it.

Grenville had left her soon after 03.00, and she hated him going, but both had agreed he must return to his room for appearances' sake.

She ran her fingers through her silky hair.

What a lover! The best ever!

She arched her body, longing for him to be by her side, and longing for him to take her yet again.

What a lover!

For some minutes, she lay still and re-lived the events of the night. Perfect! And it must be repeated and repeated and repeated! This wonderful man must be her husband! She now couldn't bear the thought of ever being parted from him. He had everything: looks, intelligence, talents, and was magnificent as a lover!

Hooked! she told herself and laughed. Yes ... and why not? He loved her as fiercely as she loved him. She knew it by the way he looked at her and had caressed her. Of course she must be careful. She mustn't rush this. He was English, and there was this reserve about him. He was certain to have a stupid bias that as she was so rich, he shouldn't marry her, but this, she felt sure, she could handle.

But certainly not in the Carlton Hotel.

She turned on her side as she thought, then suddenly, she smiled. Of course! The villa in Castagnola! The perfect love nest: away from the prying eyes of the press ... Chris and herself. Nothing could be more perfect!

Herman Rolfe had always liked to spend a month or so in Switzerland and had bought a villa, owned by a successful American movie producer, just outside Lugano, with a wonderful view of the lake. It was in this villa that Archer had unsuccessfully tried to blackmail her, but that was now in the past. It was the ideal place for a discreet love affair.

Her mind became active. There were things to arrange. First, she would need someone discreet to run the villa. The local women would gossip. Then she smiled and hugged her pillow.

Hinkle!

That tubby, kindly man who had looked after Herman Rolfe for over fifteen years, and who had now transferred his loyalty to her, and who was almost like a father figure to her.

Of course, Hinkle!

She snatched up the telephone receiver and asked the concierge to find out details of a flight from Miami to Geneva, and another flight from Nice to Geneva.

Then breaking the connection, she called Signor Transel who looked after the Castagnola villa. She told him to have the villa opened and cleaned, saying she would be arriving the day after tomorrow. Signor Transel said he would arrange it immediately.

She then ordered coffee.

The concierge called, giving her times of the two flights, and she told him to book a single from Miami and two from Nice.

Her coffee arrived.

She called the hotel operator and asked her to connect her with her residence in Paradise City. The operator said it would take only a few minutes.

Helga drank her coffee, lit a cigarette and waited, thinking of Grenville.

The telephone bell rang.

'I have your residence on the line, madame,' the operator said.

'Hinkle?' Helga said excitedly.

'Yes, Madame. I trust you are well.'

She stifled a giggle. This was so like Hinkle.

'I'm marvellous! I have news!'

'Indeed, madame?' His fruity, bishop's voice came clearly to her. 'It would seem it is good news.'

'I am in love, Hinkle!'

There was a pause, then Hinkle said, 'That would appear to be excellent news, madame.'

'I have found a man I want to marry!'

Again a pause, then Hinkle said, 'I trust this gentleman is worthy of you, madame.'

She laughed.

'Oh, Hinkle, don't be so stuffy! He's marvellous! Now listen. I have arranged to have the Castagnola villa opened. I want to stay there for a week or two, so I can get to know Mr. Grenville better . . . do you understand?'

'Certainly, madame, and you would like me to be with you.'

'Yes! Drop everything. I've booked you a flight.' Picking up the paper on which she had made notes, she read out to him the flight number and time of departure.

'Certainly, madame. I will be at the Geneva airport the day after tomorrow at 22.30.'

'Mr. Grenville and I will be arriving a little later. Oh, Hinkle, I'm so happy!' She blew a kiss in the air.

'Then I am happy for you, madame.'

She hung up.

Now for a car.

She called the Rolls-Royce agent in Lugano.

'I want a Rolls,' she said, after she had introduced herself.

'You are fortunate, Madame Rolfe, we have just had delivery of the new Camargue. It is truly a magnificent car: two tone, silver and black.'

'I want it! I shall be arriving at Geneva airport at 22.30 the day after tomorrow. Please contact Signor Transel, who is my agent in Lugano. He will arrange all that is necessary.'

'The car will be waiting for you, madame, at the airport.'

Herman Rolfe's magic key!

Chris! Dear Chris! How she longed for him to be with her now! Two more days, and they would be utterly together, safe from the press, just he, she and Hinkle!

'Relax, Chris,' Archer said soothingly. 'Things are going our way.'

They were sitting in a shabby bistro on the rue de Canada.

'You can say that!' Grenville said explosively, 'but I have to live with her! God! She is now so possessive! She is like a female spider who eats her male!'

'Come! come!' Archer spoke sharply. 'You and I will make a million each out of her. You must expect to work for it. So far you have done a wonderful job, but there is still more for you to do. Before she is completely hooked, she has to imagine you want to marry her.'

Grenville stiffened.

'Marry her?'

'I will leave it to you to convey the impression you want to be her husband,' Archer said. 'I know Helga. She is lonely: she has fallen for you, and once she believes you will marry her, we have a hook in her that will not come out.'

Grenville had already told him that Helga was taking him to the villa at Castagnola for two weeks and Archer was delighted.

'It couldn't be more perfect. That's why I am telling you things are going our way. How well do I know that villa!' He eyed Grenville. 'So she has given you some money?'

'She forced it on me. She told me to go out and buy clothes!'

'Well, you will need clothes. Don't sound so annoyed. After all, you did tell me you are a professional gigolo, didn't you?' Archer smiled. 'How much did she give you?'

'A hundred thousand francs!'

Archer nodded.

'Helga is always generous to her lovers. It is a little exaggerated, but after all, she is worth millions.' He paused, his eyes sharp. 'I need money, Chris, if I am to carry out my plan. Suppose you give me fifty thousand?'

'Suppose you tell me about this plan you keep hinting about?' Grenville demanded.

'Yes, of course.' Archer sat back in his chair. 'It is really quite simple: all good plans should be simple. After three days in the Castagnola villa, and after you have convinced Helga you want to marry her, and after you have screwed her blind, if you will excuse the coarse expression, you will be kidnapped and held to ransom, and the ransom will be two million dollars.'

Grenville gaped at him.

'Have you gone out of your mind? Me? Kidnapped?'

'This will be a faked kidnapping, but the ransom won't be faked,' Archer said. 'I know Helga. Once you have convinced her you want to marry her, we have her exactly where we want her. Consider the situation. Everything is wonderful: love, marriage, no longer lonely. She will be spinning like a top, then suddenly you are kidnapped. If she doesn't pay two million dollars, she will never see you again. She has so much money, to get you back she won't hesitate. We collect the two million: one for you and one for me. What do you think?'

'Well, for God's sake!' Grenville looked stunned. 'Suppose she goes to the police?'

'She won't. I assure you, I shall so frighten her that she will not go to the police. I know Helga. She'll pay.'

'So, she pays, then what?'

'As soon as I have the money, we leave Switzerland. Again, I repeat I know Helga. Once she realizes she has been taken for a sucker, her pride won't let her cry "thief!" '

'How will she pay this money?' Grenville asked.

'A good point. She and I are old enemies. Once you have been kidnapped, I shall call on her. It will give me the greatest pleasure. I have a numbered account in a private Swiss bank. She will pay this money to this account, and I shall transfer half to you.'

'But who is going to do the kidnapping?' Grenville asked uneasily.

'That I am going to arrange. I have a good contact in Geneva. Don't worry about that.' Archer looked at his watch. 'Now, give me fifty thousand francs. I must be on my way to Geneva in an hour.'

Grenville hesitated, then took a bundle of French francs from his pocket. He gave Archer half the bundle and Archer stuffed the bills into his pocket.

'From Geneva, I shall go to Lugano,' Archer said. 'I shall be staying at the Hotel de Suisse. Contact me there. Your job is to convince her you can't live without her. Leave everything else to me.' He smiled at Grenville. 'Kidnapping is very fashionable these days. She won't be suspicious. When it happens, don't act brave. Put up a little show of resistance, but nothing more. It will happen unexpectedly. You will be taken from the villa, and after that, all you will have to do is to keep me company until we get the money.'

'This worries me,' Grenville said uneasily. 'I have done a few shabby deals in the past, but I've never gone so far as to do anything criminal.'

'This is not criminal, Chris.' Archer got to his feet. 'The police won't come into it. Think what you will be able to do with a million dollars. With that kind of money you will be free of all those old, rich women. Love her, Chris: that's your job. The more she needs you, the easier it will be to get the money from her.'

Grenville drew in a deep breath.

'All right. When will it be?'

'Three days after you have settled in at the villa, but we will meet again before then. I will let you know what I have arranged.' Archer paused, his eyes turning bleak. 'She outsmarted me once, now it is my turn.'

CHAPTER FOUR

SOME two years ago, when Jack Archer had been a senior partner of a reputable firm of international lawyers in Lausanne, he had received a telephone call.

A harsh American voice said, 'This is Moses Seigal talking. You know me?'

Archer always read the *Herald Tribune,* so he knew Moses Seigal was one of the important Mafia men, and was being hunted by the F.B.I. for tax evasion.

'Yes, Mr. Seigal,' he said cautiously. 'I have read about you.'

'Yeah. Now listen, I want your advice and I'll pay. A guy who gives advice to a guy as big as Herman Rolfe is my idea of a guy. I'll be at Bernie's restaurant, Geneva, at eight o'clock tomorrow night. You be there, and you'll pick up some dough,' and he hung up.

For some minutes Archer hesitated. He knew Seigal was on the run, but he also knew the Mafia people were dangerous to refuse. So, without telling his partners, who would have been dismayed, he decided it might be profitable to himself personally, to talk to this man.

Bernie's restaurant was on a side street off Quai Gustave. It looked unimpressive, dark and shabby.

Entering, Archer had been greeted by a short, thickset, swarthy-looking man with a beard, who had told him Mr. Seigal was waiting.

The bearded man, introducing himself as Bernie, had taken Archer through the crowded restaurant to a room at the back where a fat, beetle-browed Italian was drinking Campari soda.

'Okay, Bernie,' the man growled. 'Get us some of your swill. I'm in a hurry.'

He waved Archer to a chair.

'I ain't got long,' he said as Archer settled himself. 'I've got a load of hot money. I want to stash it. What do I do?'

Bernie came in with two plates of spaghetti, drenched in tomato sauce, plonked them down and went away.

A little shaken, Archer said, 'In cash or bonds?'

'In cash.'

Seigal began to attack the spaghetti, eating like an animal.

'I could arrange for you to have a numbered account in a reliable private bank,' Archer said.

'Yeah. That's what I heard. Okay, you fix it. I got the money right here.' Seigal nodded to a battered suitcase by his side. 'Two and a half million bucks.'

Archer flinched.

'Yes, Mr. Seigal, I can arrange that'

'You get fifty thousand Swiss francs. Okay?'

This would go straight into Archer's pocket. He had no intention of sharing it with his partners.

'That is perfectly okay with me, Mr. Seigal.'

'So it's fixed, huh?' Seigal was eating as he talked. Spaghetti fell from his mouth, and Archer thought he was utterly revolting. 'You take the dough, huh?' He belched, then again crammed spaghetti into his mouth. 'I had you investigated, Archer. You're an all right guy, but if you think you can walk off with my dough, think again. My boys would take care of you.'

'There's no question of that,' Archer said stiffly. 'Leave the money with me, and I will arrange it. Give me an address where I can send the account number.'

Seigal nodded.

'To my wife. Here . . .' He took out his billfold and produced a stack of Swiss francs and a card. 'That's the address, and there's your pay-off.' By now, he had almost demolished the spaghetti which Archer hadn't touched. He looked at his watch. 'I've got to get moving.'

Bernie came in.

'Want some more, Moses?'

'Haven't the time. My goddamn plane is about to take

off. Hey, Bernie, look at this guy. His name is Jack Archer. He's taking care of my money. He does me a favour: you do him a favour, huh?' Turning to Archer, he went on. 'Bernie is Mr. Fix-it in this town. Anything you want done, talk to him: he'll fix it. Right, Bernie?'

'If you say so, Moses, it is so,' Bernie said.

And Archer remembered.

Leaving Geneva airport, he told the taxi driver to take him to Bernie's restaurant. As he sat in the taxi, he remembered how he had taken the two and a half million dollars to a bank and had deposited them. The director of the bank knew him, so there was no problem. He had sent the number of the account to Seigal's wife. Two months later, he read in the *Herald Tribune* that Moses Seigal had been shot to death.

Paying off the taxi, Archer walked into the shabby restaurant. There was Bernie, standing behind the bar, slightly older, slightly heavier, who recognized him and came to him, offering a hard, sweaty hand.

'Mr. Archer!'

'Hello, Bernie.'

'Come and have some spaghetti.' Bernie led Archer into the back room. 'And a bottle of Valpolicella,' and he went away.

The wine and the spaghetti arrived.

'Bernie, sit down. I want to talk to you,' Archer said, and began to eat the spaghetti, for he was hungry.

'Why else should you come?' Bernie laughed. 'You heard about Moses? He had it coming: if not his enemies, then the cops.'

'I read about it.'

Bernie went over to close the door, then sat opposite Archer.

'It is good?'

Archer stirred the sauce into the spaghetti.

'Very good. Bernie . . . I have a small problem. You could help.'

'If I can, I will.'

71

'I want to hire two reliable men. When I say reliable, I mean two men who will be paid to do a job, and then forget they have done it.'

Bernie nodded.

'What's the job, Mr. Archer?'

'I want these two men to fake – and I repeat fake – a kidnapping. The man who is to be kidnapped, has asked me to arrange this. Between you and me, he wants to frighten the woman he is living with. All these two men have to do is to arrive at the home of this woman, look menacing, hustle the man out, and drive him away. The police won't come into it. It is really a joke on the woman.'

Bernie reached for a wooden toothpick and began to explore his teeth.

'So what happens, then?' he asked.

'That's it. The woman will believe her boy friend has been kidnapped. He will keep away from her for a couple of days, then return.' Archer shrugged. 'He thinks he will bring her to heel.'

Bernie nodded.

'How about money, Mr. Archer?'

'For finding two reliable men, I will pay you five hundred francs. I will arrange payment with the two men when I have met them.'

Bernie continued to dig into his teeth for a long moment, then he shook his head.

'No, Mr. Archer, it will cost a little more. For one thousand francs, I can find two reliable men.'

Archer was in no position to bargain.

'Very well: a thousand francs.'

Bernie smiled.

'Enjoy your meal, Mr. Archer. I'll fix it,' and getting up, he left Archer alone.

By the time Archer had finished the spaghetti and the bottle of wine, Bernie returned.

'It is fixed, Mr. Archer,' he said as he dropped his bulk into the chair opposite Archer. 'These two men: I know them. They hang out here in the evenings. They are most reliable. Their work isn't much.' He shrugged his shoulders. 'They work together on the tourist steamers, and they speak English. Naturally, they are eager for money. The young one is Jacques Belmont. The older one is Max Segetti. There is a homo relationship between them.' Bernie smiled. 'I assure you, Mr. Archer, if you are willing to pay, they can be relied on.'

Archer nodded.

'I want to see and talk to them.'

'Of course, Mr. Archer. You talk to them, and if they aren't satisfactory, tell me, and I will look for two other men.'

'They are here now?'

'Sure. In the evening, this is their home.' Bernie regarded Archer, and Archer, taking the hint, produced a thousand franc bill. 'A friend of Moses,' Bernie went on, slipping the bill into his pocket, 'is a friend of mine.'

He went to the door and jerked his thumb.

Two men came into the room. One was tall, thin, with hair down to his shoulders. His white face was narrow, his eyes close set. His companion was bulky, older than the other by ten years. His dyed, straw-coloured hair looked like a disturbed bird's next. His fat face was featureless, but the small, black eyes were probing.

They were both wearing shabby jeans and dirty sweat shirts. They came to the table and stood looking at Archer. He didn't like the look of either of them, but Moses Seigal had said Bernie was to be relied on. One had, he told himself, to make do with the tools one was given.

'Sit down,' he said.

They sat down.

'I'm Segetti,' the fat man said. 'He's Belmont.'

'Bernie tells me you two are reliable.' Archer put on his tough expression. 'You had better be! A friend of mine wants to be kidnapped to frighten some sense into his girl friend. There is no question of the police coming into this. It is a joke against his girl friend, but it has to look convincing. Your job will be to rush into the villa, take the man – he will

73

put up no resistance – then drive him to another villa and leave him there. That's all you have to do. You will forget the whole thing, and return to Geneva. The villa is outside Lugano.'

Segetti nodded.

'Bernie told us it would be all right. It's fine with us.' He leaned forward, his little black eyes glistening. 'How much?'

'Shall we say two thousand francs each?' Archer said.

Segetti looked sad.

'Not quite enough, Mr. Archer. We will lose work, leaving Geneva. We could lose our jobs. I think five thousand each would be better.'

'Four thousand each, and not a franc more,' Archer said curtly.

The two men looked at each other.

'Right,' Segetti said, 'but all expenses?'

'Yes.'

'And half now?'

'No. A thousand francs each now, the rest when you have done the job.' Archer produced two one thousand franc bills and put them on the table. Segetti picked up the bills and put them in his pocket.

'I want you to wear hoods. You must look frightening,' Archer went on. 'And guns, of course. Is that a problem?'

Segetti smiled.

'Hoods and guns are no problem. I understand what you want.'

'The kidnapping will be in three days' time: that is on the evening of the 18th. I want you two to be at the Hotel de Suisse, Lugano at 14.00 on the 18th. I'll be staying there. We will finalize all the details when we meet. Bring the guns and the hoods with you. Is that understood?'

Segetti nodded.

'You have a car?'

Segetti nodded again.

Archer produced a five hundred franc bill.

'This will take care of your expenses. So it is agreed: we meet at the Hotel de Suisse, Lugano at 14.00 on the 18th.'

'It is agreed,' Segetti said, pocketing the five hundred franc bill.

While they had been talking, Archer had become more and more aware that Segetti's companion had said nothing, but had sat, staring down at his hands.

'And you, Belmont? Is it agreed?' Archer asked, a snap in his voice.

'Jacques always agrees when I agree,' Segetti said quickly. Both men got to their feet. 'Then we see you later, Mr. Archer.' With a little wave of his hand, he walked from the room, followed by Belmont.

Bernie came into the room.

'Is it satisfactory, Mr. Archer?'

'I think so. Look, Bernie, I did a good job for Seigal,' Archer said. 'He assured me you fixed things. I'm relying on you. Are you absolutely sure these two men can be relied on?'

'Cross my heart and cut my throat. Don't worry about a thing, Mr. Archer. You pay them fair, and they will deliver.'

Archer, still uneasy, got to his feet.

'They are getting eight thousand francs for less than an hour's work. Do you call that fair?'

Bernie nodded.

'That's big money for them. Yes, Mr. Archer, you have no problems.'

Archer shook hands.

'Could you get me a taxi?'

'There's one right outside, Mr. Archer. I hope to see you again.'

When Archer had driven away, Segetti and Belmont came out of the toilet where they had been waiting for Archer to go.

'What goes on?' Segetti asked, joining Bernie at the bar.

'This could be an interesting and very profitable set-up,' Bernie said. 'This fat fink, Archer, once worked for Herman Rolfe who was loaded with the stuff. Keep in touch with me, Max. I want to know who this guy is who wants to be kidnapped, and I want to know who his girl friend is. As soon as you know where the kidnapping is to take place, telephone me. Understand?'

Segetti nodded.

'We'll want hoods and guns.'

'Is that so terrible?' Bernie grinned. 'I've got hoods and guns. What I want is information.'

As Helga, followed by Grenville, walked through the Geneva customs, she saw Hinkle waiting at the barrier.

Although only fifty-two years of age, Hinkle looked considerably older. He was short, rotund and balding. White wisps of hair softened his florid complexion. He had had the thankless task of nursing Herman Rolfe, a polio victim, for fifteen years. When Rolfe had died, Hinkle had transferred his loyalty to Helga, whom he admired.

The news she had told him that she was in love disturbed him. He was well aware of her weakness for men, but seeing her approach, looking radiant, he thought hopefully this could be, at last, the real thing, but then, looking beyond her at Grenville, he had immediate doubts. This tall, too handsome, too suave man sent up a red light in Hinkle's mind.

'Dear Hinkle!' Helga said, grasping his hand. 'How I have missed you!' Turning to Grenville, she went on, 'Chris, this is Hinkle whom I have told you about.'

Grenville had no time for servants. He nodded distantly, then said, 'The luggage, Helga. Perhaps he will take care of it,' and gave Hinkle the luggage stubs as if conveying a favour.

'Yes, sir,' Hinkle said.

From that moment, they were enemies.

Hinkle turned to Helga.

'The new Rolls is just outside, madame. If you will give me a few minutes,' then snapping his fingers at a waiting porter, he walked away.

'Chris, darling,' Helga said. 'Please ... Hinkle is very special. Do be nice to him.'

Realizing he had made a *faux pas*, Grenville said hurriedly, 'Sorry. Of course.'

They went together from the airport lobby to where the Camargue Rolls stood waiting.

'Some car,' Grenville said, impressed.

Helga walked around the Rolls and then clapped her hands.

'It's really marvellous!' She got in the rear seat and as Grenville joined her, she took his hand. 'Oh, Chris! This is really when I appreciate the power of money! I'm so lucky! And now . . . you and I . . . I know you will love the villa.'

Within a few minutes, Hinkle slid under the driving wheel, the luggage in the boot.

'Is all well at Paradise City, Hinkle?' Helga asked.

'Yes, madame. The garden is looking very well.'

'I told Transel to prepare the villa.'

'So I understand, madame. Whilst waiting for your arrival, I telephoned him. All is in order.'

Helga patted Grenville's hand.

'You see how Hinkle takes care of me.'

'And madame,' Hinkle went on, 'as it is so late, I have booked rooms at the Trois Couronnes Hotel at Vevey for tonight.'

'Thank you.' Helga turned to Grenville. 'It is a five hour drive from Vevey to Castagnola. We shall arrive tomorrow in time for lunch. Hinkle, what about food?'

'I have given Transel instructions, madame. He will stock the deep freeze.'

Helga sighed and rested her head on Grenville's shoulder. She relaxed as the Rolls took them along the lakeside and towards Vevey.

At the Trois Couronnes, Helga said good night to Grenville, pressed his hand, her eyes alight with promises, and then was escorted to her room. As soon as he was in his room, Grenville put through a call to Archer at the Hotel de Suisse in Lugano.

'It's all arranged,' Archer told him. 'There is nothing for you to worry about. In three days, the operation will begin.'

'I'm not so sure there is nothing to worry about,' Grenville said, uneasily. 'This man of hers . . . Hinkle . . . worries me.'

77

'Hinkle?' Archer's voice shot up. 'Is he here?'

'He's very much here, and very much in charge. He took one look at me and hated me. I know the signs. These ghastly old family retainers can be deadly.'

'Yes.' Archer, in his turn, became worried. 'Hinkle, like Helga, is nobody's fool.'

'Well, it's your funeral. You work it out.'

'It'll work out. Love her, Chris. That's your job. She will override Hinkle once she is sure you want to marry her. I'll look after the rest.'

'Just as long as you do,' said Grenville, who was now in a surly mood.

'Be careful how you handle Hinkle,' Archer went on. 'Be nice to him: flatter him. Don't overdo it, Chris, but pour oil.'

So the following morning, Grenville came from the hotel to where Hinkle was dusting the Rolls.

'Hello, Hinkle,' Grenville said in his smoothest manner. 'That's really a beautiful car. Tell me about it.'

'I would say, sir, it is the best car in the world,' Hinkle said coldly.

'An entirely new line. The Silver Shadow doesn't compare with it. I always prefer a two-door job.'

'The body work is of the master stylist, Pininfarina. This model is the first to use the latest Lucas Opus electronic ignition.'

Not knowing what Hinkle was talking about, Grenville wandered around the car.

'I suppose it eats petrol?'

'When one is fortunate to own a car like this, sir, one must expect it to use petrol,' Hinkle said, still cold and aloof.

'Yes.' Grenville turned on all his charm. 'Madame Rolfe tells me how well you look after her, Hinkle. I too want to look after her.'

Hinkle regarded him, his fat face expressionless.

'Yes, Mr. Grenville.'

Trying again, Grenville said, 'I want to make her happy as I know you make her happy.'

That didn't get him anywhere for Hinkle opened the boot of the car and put away the feather duster.

Grenville realized he had a problem on his hands. Hinkle was definitely hostile.

Then Helga appeared.

'Do we go?' She went up to Grenville and kissed him lightly on his cheek. 'Hinkle? No problems?'

'The luggage is in the boot. We can leave when you wish, madame.'

'Then let's go. Chris! I can't wait to show you my Swiss home!'

Some ten years ago, Herman Rolfe had bought the villa at Castagnola, just outside Lugano, from an American movie producer.

The villa had everything that an imaginative and rich movie producer could devise: an indoor heated swimming pool, an outdoor swimming pool and a vast terrace overlooking Lugano and the lake. There were four bedrooms, each with de luxe bathrooms; sauna baths, servants' quarters, a tiny elevator that conveyed logs from the cellar to the big fireplace, two chair lifts that took you to the main highway if you wanted to go for a walk and didn't want to descend the hundred and fifty steps through the garden which was floodlit at night. There was a kitchen with its push-button miracles, fully equipped to produce dinner for some twenty people. The stereo radio and gramophone could produce music in every room if you pressed the right button. Every room had a colour TV set. There was a deep freeze cabinet run by its own generator so electrical cuts didn't matter. Speaker-boxes wired to every telephone throughout the villa allowed you to talk to anyone in any city in the world without moving from your chair, so finely tuned you could hear someone breathing in Tokyo or anywhere else in the world. There was also a movie projection room with twenty plush seats and a vista-vision screen.

Grenville was fascinated as Helga happily showed him around.

They had had lunch on the way. Hinkle had gone to the kitchen. The rooms were ready.

Helga led Grenville to her bedroom.

It was a beautiful room with apricot-coloured leather padded walls, mirrors, a fitted white wool carpet and fumed oak fittings. The king-sized bed dominated the room.

'Chris, darling!' Helga said. 'Hinkle understands. We sleep here!'

Grenville, feeling a little stifled by so much luxury in spite of what he had been used to, asked if he could take a swim.

'The pool, Helga! It's marvellous. Could I?'

'You are free to do what you like, Chris. This is your home!'

She left him, humming under her breath, and went into the kitchen where Hinkle, wearing a white coat, was preparing dinner.

'Hinkle! I'm so happy!' she exclaimed. 'Isn't he wonderful?'

'He would appear so, madame,' Hinkle said in his lower tone.

Helga laughed.

'Oh, Hinkle! I want to marry him! But you will always be with us.'

'I trust so, madame.'

Laughing, she caught hold of him and whirled him away in an old-fashioned waltz. Without touching her, Hinkle followed her steps and they danced around the kitchen, then she kissed his cheek and left him. His fat face sad, Hinkle began to cut up a chicken.

In her bedroom, Helga threw off her clothes, put on a bathing cap, covered her nakedness with a wrap, and ran down the stairs to the bathing pool.

Grenville was lazily floating, his eyes closed.

Helga dived in, swam under him, surfaced and then dragged him down under the water. Startled, Grenville broke free, spluttering to see Helga, naked, swimming with the ease and speed of a dolphin. He saw at once he was way out of her class so he moved to the side of the pool and watched her.

What a magnificent swimmer! he thought as she did four lengths at a speed that made him envious, then she came to him and entwined her arms and legs around him. Her mouth found his and his hands slid down her body, pulling her hard against him.

Later, they sat on the terrace, watching the sunset. As the sky turned to a fierce furnace red, Helga took Grenville's hand.

'I have always hoped to find someone like you, Chris,' she said.

'But it's no good, darling,' Grenville said, moving into his act. 'It is marvellous now, but for how long?'

'What do you mean?' She looked searchingly at him.

'You and I.' Grenville wondered how many times he had made this speech. 'It is not possible, Helga. This moment of loveliness will go. If you weren't so rich . . .'

She took her hand from his and turned to look directly at him. That direct stare bothered him.

'Explain yourself, Chris!' The snap in her voice warned him he wasn't dealing with some stupid old woman.

'Surely, Helga, it is obvious. If you weren't so rich, I would ask you to marry me. That would give me the greatest of all happiness, but Englishmen just don't live on their wives.'

'I've never heard such nonsense!' Helga said. 'Who said you had to live on me? You have many talents. You and I, working together, could make a terrific combination.'

Grenville moved uneasily.

'I do have talents, but I have never been able to make money. This would only bring unhappiness to both of us. Let us enjoy these few moments of bliss, then I'll go. I honestly . . .'

'Chris! Pull yourself together! You are talking like a goddamn ham actor,' Helga said sharply. 'Your dialogue is utter corn. We are talking about love, not money!' She looked fixedly at him. 'I love you! Now tell me: do you love me?'

Into Grenville's mind flashed the thought: God! This woman is dangerous! All the other old bitches I fed that talk to lapped it up. Here, she is telling me I'm talking corn!

'Love you? Can you ask?' His fertile brain was working furiously. 'I think you are the most marvellous . . .'

'Never mind that!' Helga snapped. 'I want to know: do you or don't you love me?'

Grenville drew in a deep breath. He realized he was trapped, and there was no way out.

'Helga, darling, I love you.'

Helga studied him for a few moments while he gave her his most sincere expression, then she relaxed back in her chair and smiled at him.

'Then we have no problem. It's time we had a drink.' She reached out for the bell push on the table and pressed it.

Hinkle appeared on the terrace, carrying a silver tray on which stood a big shaker and two glasses. As he set the tray on the table, he said, 'Perhaps Mr. Grenville would prefer something else. This is vodka martini, madame.'

'Fine with me,' Grenville said, and how he now longed for a drink!

As Hinkle poured, he said, 'Dinner will be in half an hour, madame.'

'What are you giving us?' Helga asked, taking the glass he offered.

'It has been a little rushed, madame, but tonight, *pâté de foie gras* and *chicken à la King*.'

Helga looked at Grenville.

'You could have a steak if you would prefer it.'

'Oh, no. Hinkle's menu sounds perfect.'

Hinkle inclined his head.

'Then in half an hour, madame. As it is a fine evening, you will prefer, no doubt, to dine on the terrace.'

'Lovely!'

While Hinkle set the table, neither Helga nor Grenville talked. They sat watching the sun slowly sink, sipping their drinks.

When Hinkle returned to the kitchen, Helga said, 'We

will have a serious talk after dinner, Chris. Let's forget it for now,' and she went on to discuss what they would do the following day. 'It would be fun to drive up into the mountains. There is an amusing little bistro where we can lunch. It would give Hinkle time to rest. I am sure he will give us one of his wonderful omelettes for supper.'

Grenville said that would be fine. He was now depressed. He found Helga overpowering. At least, he told himself, he had hinted at marriage, and that was what Archer wanted him to do.

With Hinkle hovering over them, they ate an excellent dinner. Then they moved from the table and sat in lounging chairs, looking at the lake, now like a silver mirror in the moonlight.

Hinkle served coffee and brandy and then cleared the table.

'Hinkle! Go to bed!' Helga said. 'We have everything we need. Mr. Grenville will lock up. You must be very tired.'

'Thank you, madame, if you are sure there is nothing further, then I will retire.'

'Nothing, and thank you for a wonderful dinner. Have a good night's rest.'

'And I trust you will too, madame,' Hinkle said and carried the tray into the kitchen.

'I really don't know what I would do without him,' Helga said. 'He is part of my life.'

'Yes.' Grenville lit a cigarette. 'I can well imagine.'

There was a pause, then Helga said, 'Let us now talk seriously about ourselves, Chris. Let us be absolutely frank. I will begin. I married Herman for what I could get out of him. He was a cripple and impotent with not a shred of kindness in him. He wanted a good-looking, clever hostess to run his various establishments, and I fitted his requirements. There was to be no cheating, but I did cheat. I have this thing which is a curse. I need a man.' She smiled at him and patted his hand. 'I am so sick of sordid affairs I want a permanent man. I have never been in love before, but I am now ... with you.'

Startled by her frankness, Grenville said, 'I love you too, Helga, but there is this thing in me that will not allow me to live on a woman. You are too rich.'

'All right, I have to respect that,' Helga said. 'Now tell me something: if I gave all my money away, would you marry me?'

Grenville stared at her.

'But you couldn't possibly do such a thing!'

'Never mind what I could or couldn't do!' Again there was a snap in her voice. 'The question is would you marry me if I had the same amount of money as you had?'

Again feeling trapped, Grenville touched her hand.

'Of course I would.'

She smiled at him.

'Don't look so worried. I am not going to do anything so stupid as to give away my husband's magic key. It unlocks so many doors. So ... as I don't intend to descend to your financial level, you must ascend to mine. If you were worth five million dollars which you had earned and which belonged to you, would you marry me?'

Grenville ran his fingers through his hair.

'Helga! Do stop this! I could never make five million dollars!'

'I will show you how you could make them.'

Grenville stared incredulously at her.

'How?'

'By using your talents. I will make you a senior partner in my corporation. We are setting up a factory in France, and then in Germany. With your flair, your appearance and your languages you could handle the deals. You would have accountants, experts and assistants, but you would control the deals. You would become a stockholder, and you would be on a percentage basis. I promise you, this would be no gift. You will earn every dollar you make, but I know, in three or four years' time, you would be worth five million dollars. I would lend you this money at six per cent interest. It would be yours.' She smiled at him. 'We could get married tomorrow.'

The very thought of working in an office with Helga, driving him on, with accountants and experts crowding him, made Grenville inwardly shudder.

'It's wonderful of you, Helga, but frankly, I couldn't cope. It's not my thing,' he said earnestly. 'It is a marvellous offer, but ...'

'Of course, you could cope with it!' There was now steel in Helga's voice. 'You would have me behind you, and the whole of my organization. We could have marvellous fun.'

Then Grenville remembered Archer's advice: love her.

'This is terribly exciting, Helga.' He got to his feet. 'Would you let me think about it? May we sleep on it? I'm almost convinced, as long as you would be with me to help me, but seeing you, in the moonlight, looking so lovely, I want to love you.'

'Oh, Chris!' Helga gave him her hand. 'Yes, let's make love.'

He put his arm around her, and together they walked across the terrace into the living-room.

'Darling, will you close the shutters? I'll be waiting for you. Hurry!'

As Grenville wound down the shutters, Helga walked happily to her bedroom.

At exactly 08.30, the following morning, Hinkle entered Helga's bedroom, pushing the breakfast trolley before him. As he began to draw the curtains Helga came awake, and immediately became aware that Grenville was not at her side.

'Where is Mr. Grenville?' she asked sharply.

'He is taking a swim, madame.'

'Oh.' Helga relaxed. She sat up in bed and fluffed up her hair. 'Coffee! You are always so punctual, Hinkle.'

'Yes, madame. It is a beautiful morning. I trust you slept well.'

Helga laughed.

'Marvellously!'

Hinkle pushed the trolley to the bedside.

'Will you be in for lunch, madame?'

'No. We are going into the mountains and we won't be back until four or five. If we could have an omelette for dinner?'

'Certainly, madame.'

He left her, and Helga drank her coffee, thinking about Grenville. His love-making had been marvellous. She felt sure now that she could persuade him to take an important position in her corporation. She wouldn't want to be married in Lugano. She would want the marriage to take place in Paradise City. To launch Grenville, it would have to be a big affair, and the thought thrilled her.

They would fly to Paradise City at the end of the week. The announcement would be made. There would be a lot to arrange. She wondered how Loman and Winborn would react. Then she frowned. She suddenly remembered she had gone off with Chris without telling Winborn or Loman where she was! She also remembered she had left most of her clothes at the Plaza Athénée Hotel.

Winborn might even imagine she had been kidnapped! Jumping out of bed, she took a quick shower and then slipped into a trouser suit.

As she left the bedroom, Grenville, wrapped in a towel, came towards her.

'Darling!' Helga ran to him and they kissed. 'Did you have a lovely swim?'

'Marvellous.'

'I've just remembered ... I haven't told my people I am here. Ask Hinkle for coffee and sit on the terrace. I won't be long.'

Leaving him, she went into the living-room and reached for the telephone.

Grenville went to his bedroom and put on slacks and a polo neck sweater, then went out onto the terrace.

'Tea or coffee, sir?' Hinkle asked, suddenly appearing.

'Coffee, please ... nothing else.'

Grenville sat down. Faintly, he could hear Helga talking

on the telephone. He must gain a little time, he told himself. He must see Archer. But how?

While swimming, he had considered Helga's proposal. He was sure, even in four years' time, he would not be capable of earning five million dollars. No, he must first try for the million dollars Archer was promising him. If that didn't work, then maybe he would have to think again, but, first, he must see Archer.

Hinkle brought the coffee.

'Is there a golf course near here?' Grenville asked.

'Yes, sir: a reasonable one, I understand. It is at Ponte Tresa. I have a map if you would care to look at it.'

'Thanks, I would.'

He had finished his coffee and had studied the map before Helga appeared. She looked irritated.

'I'm going to be held up,' she said, sitting by his side. 'My stupid people are making a mess of buying the site at Versailles.' She put her hand on his. 'That's why you are going to be so important to me. You and I, working together, won't make a mess! I was planning to go into the mountains, but, now I must stay here for more telephone calls.'

Here was Grenville's chance.

'I understand.' He smiled at her. 'Helga, darling, about last night's talk. May I have just a little time? Would you mind if I have a game of golf? When playing golf, I think better than at any other time, and I will be back with an answer.' He smiled. 'I think the answer must be yes.'

Helga, her mind now occupied with business, nodded.

'Go ahead, darling. Take the Rolls. When do I see you?'

'I'll be back around three o'clock. Will that be all right?'

'Of course. But your clubs . . . don't you need clubs to play golf?'

Grenville laughed.

'The pro will lend me a set.' He got to his feet, bent and kissed her. 'I'll get off.'

She watched him leave, disappointed. She would have liked him to have stayed with her, to be able to consult him, to get his views on the difficulties that had arisen, and to be able to assesss his thinking, but, she told herself, there was time.

Standing on the terrace, she watched him drive away in the Rolls, then she went to her bedroom where Hinkle had just finished making the bed.

'Would it bother you to give me something light for lunch, Hinkle?' she asked. 'I have phone calls to make and Mr. Grenville is going to play golf and won't be back until after lunch.'

'Certainly, madame. I suggest a grilled sole.'

'Yes.' She wandered restlessly around the bedroom. 'Hinkle! I really love him! I'm trying to persuade him to take a position in the firm, but he is so correct. If I can persuade him, we will marry.'

'If that would make you happy, madame,' Hinkle said, in his disapproving voice and went into the bathroom.

The telephone bell began to ring, and for the next three hours, Helga was engrossed in the affairs of the Herman Rolfe Electronic Corporation.

CHAPTER FIVE

SITTING in the shabby lounge of the Hotel de Suisse, Archer thought back on the previous day. He had been busy and was satisfied. He had rented a Mercedes from the Avis people, then had gone around talking to the various estate agents until he had found a small wooden villa on the outskirts of Paradiso which is a continuation of Lugano. It was a modest place and he had been forced to rent it for a month, but it would act admirably, he told himself, as a hide-out for Grenville.

Tomorrow at 14.00, Segetti and Belmont would arrive. He would drive them to Helga's villa so that they would know where to find it and then to the rented villa. Tomorrow night the kidnapping would take place.

Archer nodded to himself. As long as Grenville had taken care of Helga, Archer could see no reason why, in a few days, he wouldn't be worth a million dollars. It was, he thought, a well worked-out plan, but everything depended on how well Grenville had done his homework.

Glancing through the dirty glass doors of the hotel that led into the street, he saw a silver and black Rolls-Royce pull up and Grenville about to get out.

Jumping to his feet, Archer hurried from the hotel, and Grenville, seeing him, opened the off-side door. Archer got into the car and Grenville set it moving.

'What a magnificent car!' Archer exclaimed, and a wave of envy ran through him. He thought if it hadn't been for Helga, by now he might just possibly have been able to buy such a car.

'I have to talk to you!' The sharp note in Grenville's voice made Archer look quickly at him.

89

'Is something wrong?'

'This woman is suffocating me! She's driving me crazy!' Grenville snapped. He edged the car through the heavy traffic until they came to the lake. He looked for parking space, but, in Lugano, parking space was practically non-existent. Muttering under his breath, he continued on, until he found a space with a no-parking sign. He pulled in and turned off the engine. 'She now wants me to work in her firm! Can you imagine? She's determined to marry me! She says she will loan me five million dollars so I won't be living on her! Who in his right mind would want to work for her? She would never leave me alone! When I wasn't screwing her, I'd be at a desk!'

Archer drew in a deep breath. If only such an offer had been made to him, he thought. How he would have jumped at it! A loan of five million dollars, and the opportunity to work with the Herman Rolfe Electronic Corporation! He regarded Grenville and suddenly had complete contempt for him. He was, indeed, a gigolo, afraid to work, afraid of responsibility.

'Yes, I understand your feelings,' he said quietly. 'But there is no need to get worked up, Chris. How have you left it?'

'I told her I wanted to think it over,' Grenville said sullenly. 'I said I thought best when I was playing golf. It was the only thing I could think of to get away from her. She is caught up with some dreary business about buying a site in Versailles so she let me go.' He banged his clenched fist on the driving wheel. 'She would marry me tomorrow if I agree to work for her!'

'But that's what we want her to think, Chris,' Archer said patiently. 'You are taking this far too seriously. There is no chance of you two getting married. You have done very well. Keep it up. When you go back, tell her you will work for her and the sooner you can marry her the happier you will be.'

Grenville took out his cigarette case and lit a cigarette.

'The thought of being married to her makes my blood run

cold. Are you sure it is going to be all right? When can you get me away from her?'

Again Archer regarded him, feeling contempt. What would he give to change places with this handsome, useless dummy?

'Tomorrow night you will be kidnapped and your worries will be over,' he said. 'Things are very definitely going our way.'

'I hope they are. You have no idea how possessive and domineering she is! I've never met such a woman.'

'Do try and relax,' Archer said soothingly. 'Everything is arranged. Tomorrow night at ten o'clock, two men will arrive, wearing hoods and carrying guns. They will threaten you both. You should put up a very minor show of resistance, but don't overdo it as these two are amateurs. Go with them. They will leave Helga a note which I have prepared. I will coach them what to say to her. I assure you they will say enough to stop her calling the police. They will drive you to a villa I have rented and I will pay them off and then I will take over. I assure you, in less than a week, you will be worth a million dollars. It is really as simple as that.'

Grenville stubbed out his cigarette in the ash-tray.

'But what about Hinkle?'

'Yes ... there's Hinkle.' Archer frowned. 'What time does he go to bed?'

'God knows! Last night Helga sent him to bed after dinner.'

'To be on the safe side, we will make the kidnapping at eleven o'clock. Suggest Hinkle leaves you two alone.'

'He may stay up.'

'Then one of my men must take care of him. And another thing, Chris, you must unlock the front door. I know the villa. There is no way to get in except through the front door. There is a loo in the vestibule. Excuse yourself, once you know Hinkle is out of the way, then unlock the front door ... understand?'

Grenville nodded.

There came a tap on the car window and both men looked

around. A policeman in a white helmet, brown uniform and jackboots was looking at them.

Exasperated and nervy, Grenville pressed the button to lower the window.

'What is it?' he barked in Italian.

'You are in a no-parking zone, sir,' the policeman said. 'I am giving you a ticket.'

'To hell with that!' Grenville snapped. 'There are no parking places in this stupid town! You people should get parking properly organized!'

Archer, who had lived in Switzerland for a long time and knew how touchy the Swiss police were, was horrified.

The policeman's eyes hardened.

'Your papers, sir.'

'Oh, for God's sake!' Grenville opened the glove compartment and gave the policeman the car's papers.

After taking some time examining the papers, the policeman again regarded Grenville.

'This is not your car?'

'You can read, can't you?' Grenville snapped. 'The car is owned by Madame Herman Rolfe. You may possibly have heard of her. She lent me the car.'

The policeman's face became stony.

'Your passport, sir.'

As Grenville travelled so much, he always carried his passport with him. He handed it to the policeman.

Then Archer made a stupid mistake. He intervened. Taking out his wallet, he produced one of his old business cards, giving his name and the address of his late firm of international lawyers.

'As you will see, officer,' he said in his smoothest manner, 'Mr. Grenville is English and is not used to continental regulations. I assure you, Madame Rolfe has lent him this car. He is staying with her as her guest.'

The policeman studied the card, then handed it back. He returned the car papers and the passport to Grenville.

'Please don't park in a no-parking zone in the future, sir,' he said, saluted and motioned Grenville to drive on.

As the Rolls drifted away, the policeman, who had an excellent memory, began to write in his notebook. He was puzzled that a man so shabbily dressed as Archer was could claim to be an international lawyer.

'The bastard!' Grenville muttered as he continued on along the lake road.

'For goodness sake, Chris!' Archer said nervously. 'You can't talk that way to a Swiss policeman. That was very stupid of you.'

'To hell with him!'

He pulled into the parking lot of the Eden Hotel.

'Let's have a drink.'

The two men walked onto the terrace and took an isolated table. They sat down and Grenville ordered two gin martinis.

'Now, look Jack, this has to come right,' he said. 'Tell me about these men who are going to kidnap me. Are you sure they are reliable?'

Archer waited until the drinks arrived, then he began to talk.

Grenville returned to the villa a little after 15.00, feeling relaxed. Archer had convinced him that in a few days he would own a million dollars with no strings attached. He had played nine holes with the pro and had beaten him so easily that the pro had generously said that Grenville was the best golfer he had ever played with and that pleased Grenville.

He drove the Rolls into the garage and then entered the villa. As he closed the front door, he could hear Helga talking on the telephone, so he went to his bedroom, took a shower, changed, then wandered into the living-room.

Helga was wearing her hard expression, but it softened at the sight of him.

'What a morning!' she said. 'These fools! They have been driving me out of my mind!' She pushed aside a mass of papers spread out on the desk and getting to her feet, she ran to him and kissed him. 'Dear Chris! Tell me the answer . . . tell me it is yes!'

'It is yes,' Grenville said and picking her up, he carried her into her bedroom and kicked the door shut. 'And we will have an immediate dress rehearsal.'

'You'll shock Hinkle!' Helga said, but she was already slipping out of her trouser suit.

'To hell with Hinkle! I have myself a wife.'

Ten minutes later, lying side by side, naked on the bed, Helga, ecstatically happy, began to tell Grenville about her wedding plans.

'We will go to Paradise City. I have a wonderful place there on an island. It's perfect. There is a cottage which you can have while I make the announcement. It must be a big, big wedding, Chris! There are so many important people and their wives, my executives and people we deal with who must be invited.'

Grenville cringed at the thought, but he gently stroked her hand.

'I am the luckiest man in the world,' he said, thinking by tomorrow evening he would be free of her, never see her again, and own a million dollars.

A gentle tap sounded on the door and Hinkle said through the door, 'Mr. Winborn is on the telephone, madame.' He spoke in his doleful, disapproving voice.

'Oh, damn the man!' Helga said furiously, but she snatched up the telephone receiver by the bed. 'What is it, Stanley?' She listened, then said, 'No! We will not pay a dollar more! This is a try-on! For God's sake, Stanley, can't you handle this instead of bothering me. I'm trying to relax.'

Grenville slid off the bed and went into the bathroom. God! he thought, to be married to this commercial machine! She was still talking when, dressed, he wandered out onto the terrace.

'Some tea, sir?' Hinkle asked, appearing.

'A double whisky and soda,' Grenville said and sat down.

Helga didn't appear for half an hour.

'I want to tell you about this deal, Chris,' she said, sitting by his side. 'You will be handling it. It is going to be big and the French government are trying to be greedy. Let me begin from the beginning . . .'

For the next hour, Grenville nearly went crazy with boredom while Helga talked figures, costs, loans, interest rates and so on. Somehow, he managed to keep an intelligent expression and nod from time to time, but the crunch came when she paused and said, 'Now you know the set-up, Chris. What is your opinion?'

Grenville flinched. He had no opinion because he had scarcely listened to what she had been saying and even if he had been listening, all this financial talk meant nothing to him.

'Before expressing an opinion, Helga,' he said carefully, 'I would like to study the papers and the figures. Would that be possible? I've warned you I'm green about finance, but I think I could be a bit intelligent if I had a couple of hours looking at the plans and the figures.'

Helga, looking disappointed, nodded.

'All right, Chris. I'll get Winborn to fly copies of the contract and figures down here right away. I can see your point.'

She reached for the telephone at her side and called Paris as Hinkle arrived with a shaker of vodka martini and glasses.

Grenville thought, At least, I've gained time!

As Hinkle poured the drinks, Helga spoke to Winborn's secretary and told her to send copies of the Versailles contract and the figures immediately.

'I want it by tomorrow,' she snapped and hung up.

'Will you be dining in, madame?' Hinkle asked.

'Let's go out, darling,' Grenville said hurriedly. He felt he had to get away from the villa and away from financial talk. 'Isn't there somewhere amusing where we could eat?'

'Of course. That's a good idea. We will go to Huguenin: it is simple, but good. No, Hinkle, we will go out.'

When Hinkle had left the terrace, Grenville, anxious to get Helga's mind off business, began asking questions about her Paradise City home. Helga was happy to give him a description of the house and time moved swiftly. A little after 20.00, she went to her bedroom to change and Grenville

95

remained on the terrace. Another twenty-seven hours, he thought.

After a good Italian-style dinner, they wandered, hand in hand along the lakeside. Helga was now relaxed, her mind at ease. This man was going to be her husband! She kept looking at him, admiring his tall, lean figure and his handsome face. She thought of the excitement of the wedding preparations. What a surprise it would be for Loman and Winborn! She wondered when she should tell them. She decided it would be wise to hold back the news until they had met Grenville and until she had told them that he would be a senior partner. She imagined they wouldn't be happy about this, but there was nothing they could do about it! She was in complete control of the corporation, holding seventy-five per cent of the shares. The other directors would also raise their eyebrows, but to hell with them! It was a little disappointing that this tall, handsome man hadn't shown any real interest in the corporation as yet, but she mustn't rush him. Working with him, she was sure she could ignite his interest.

She realized she was neglecting him so she asked about his game of golf.

Grenville too had been wandering along, thinking of tomorrow night's kidnapping, still a little uneasy about the results. He began to tell her about his game of golf with the pro, and like most golfers, he gave her a blow-by-blow account of his game, which rapidly bored Helga who thought golf a complete waste of time, but she simulated interest and said, 'Bravo!' when Grenville concluded by saying he had thoroughly beaten the pro.

Returning to the villa, they found Hinkle waiting up for them.

'Now, Hinkle,' Helga said firmly, 'in the future, after dinner, you must go to your room. I know you like TV. If there is anything I want, I will ring for you, but I do not want you to wait up for us. Is that understood?'

Hinkle inclined his head.

'Very well, madame, if that is your wish.'

'Mr. Grenville will lock up. So after dinner, please relax.'

Listening to this, Grenville drew in a sigh of relief. Maybe Archer was right when he had said everything was going their way.

Grenville came awake soon after 07.00. Helga, by his side, was sleeping.

This was the day, Grenville thought, but he had to get through twenty-two hours before he was liberated. He was sure those awful papers and accounts would arrive in a few hours. Then Helga would expect him to study them and then express an opinion. This he couldn't face. His only escape was to feign illness. This was nothing new to him. Time and again, when he could no longer bear the company of his various old women, he had pleaded migraine. It was a certain winner.

He lay still until Helga began to move, then he released a little moan. Over the years he had perfected this sighing moan that was very convincing.

Helga came awake and sat up.

'Chris? What is it?'

'Nothing.' He put his hands over his eyes. 'I didn't mean to wake you. It's just the usual damn thing.'

She leaned over him anxiously.

'Are you in pain?'

'Pain? It's migraine. Once in a while I get these attacks.' Grenville suppressed a moan. 'Look, darling, just leave me be. If I stay still, it's not all that bad.'

'Migraine! My poor darling!' Helga slid out of bed. 'I'll get you something.'

'No, please don't. I always ride it out.' He managed to sound brave. 'I'm sorry about this, but just leave me. Even talking hurts.'

'Of course, Chris. Would you like some tea? Can't I do anything for you?'

'No . . . nothing. It'll probably go away in an hour or so.'

'I'm so sorry.' Helga hesitated, then as he continued to remain still, his hands covering his eyes, she went into the bathroom, took a hasty shower, then moving silently, she dressed.

Watching her between his fingers, Grenville now and then released his little moan.

'Chris, darling . . . let me call a doctor.'

'No doctor has ever cured migraine,' Grenville said. Then with an obvious effort, he took his hands from his face. 'I'll be all right. Just leave me here, please, and darling, don't fuss.' Then he closed his eyes.

Worried and upset, Helga went onto the terrace where Hinkle was watering the flowers. Seeing her, he turned off the hose and came over to her.

'You are early, madame. Is something wrong?'

'Mr. Grenville has an attack of migraine,' Helga said. 'We mustn't disturb him.'

Hinkle's fat face became expressionless.

'Yes, madame. It is a disagreeable ailment. Will you have coffee on the terrace.'

'Yes, please.'

She drank the coffee while she worried about Grenville. As Hinkle came to take the tray away, she said, 'You wouldn't imagine a man such as Mr. Grenville could be a migraine victim, would you, Hinkle?'

Hinkle lifted his eyebrows.

'I believe it is a nervous complaint. No, madame, you wouldn't have thought so.'

Helga felt an urgent need to confide in him.

'Don't go away, Hinkle. I want to talk to you. Please sit down.'

'I would prefer to stand, madame,' Hinkle said with a slight bow.

She laughed.

'Oh, Hinkle! How correct you always are, and yet I regard you as my best friend. Please sit down.'

'Thank you, madame, and very well, madame.' Hinkle perched himself on the edge of a terrace chair.

'I must tell you! Mr. Grenville and I are going to get married,' Helga said. 'He has agreed to become a senior partner of the firm.' She drew in a happy breath. 'We plan to marry next month.'

Hinkle's expression was that of a man who had bitten into a quince, but he instantly assumed a deadpan look.

'Then may I offer my congratulations to Mr. Grenville,' he said, 'and my very best wishes to you, madame.'

'Thank you, dear Hinkle. Chris is going to make me so happy!' Helga said. 'I can no longer continue my life alone. I know you know how lonely I am. It will be marvellous to have him by my side. For me not to worry about going out alone: to be able to come alive after these dreary years with Mr. Rolfe.' She drew in a deep breath. 'Hinkle! Do understand and do approve.'

'Of course, madame,' but the disapproving note in his voice remained. He got to his feet.

'Oh, sit down!' Helga exclaimed, suddenly angry with him. 'We will leave for Paradise City at the end of this week. I want you to handle all the arrangements. It will be a big wedding.'

Hinkle remained standing.

'You may rely on me,' he said, in his lowest tone.

Helga knew Hinkle. When he was upset, nobody could do anything with him. He had to be given time.

'As long as I can always rely on you, Hinkle,' she said gently.

'Yes, madame. You may always rely on me. Now, if you would kindly excuse me, I have things to do in the villa.'

Helga watched him cross the terrace, his back stiff. If only he had been pleased, she thought, but she must give him time. She must talk to Chris. He must understand how important Hinkle was to her. Chris must make a sincere effort to win Hinkle's approval. In the past, when she had married Herman, Hinkle had disapproved of her, but she had worked on him, and finally, at the most difficult period of her life, he had proved loyal.*

Moving quietly, she went to her bedroom, gently opened the door and peered in. Grenville, who was dying for coffee and a cigarette, heard her as she turned the door handle and quickly put his hand over his eyes.

* See *The Joker in the Pack*.

Helga regarded him, then softly shut the door.

God! Grenville thought. What a hellish day this was going to be! But he must keep up this pretence until Archer's men took him away. He consoled himself by thinking of what it would mean to own a million dollars. For the first time, since Archer had so smoothly outlined his plan for the kidnapping, Grenville began seriously to think about it. He was uneasy about Helga. There was this steel fibre in her that awed and worried him. There was a possibility, in spite of Archer's glib assurances, that she could turn ugly once she realized she had been conned. Thinking about this, he decided it would be dangerous to remain in Europe once he had got his share of the money. After further thinking, he decided he would fly to the West Indies the moment Archer had given him the million dollars, charter a yacht, find some enthusiastic dolly bird and get lost. When the smoke had settled, he would then return to Europe which was his happy hunting ground.

Then a thought entered his mind that made him stiffen and frown.

Could he trust Archer? he asked himself. What did he know about Archer? They had met by chance in that depressing little hotel in Paris. Was Archer really an international lawyer? Grenville moved uneasily. Could Archer be one of these smooth con men you heard about? Admittedly, he must have known Helga. His knowledge of her proved that. Grenville thought of Archer's shabbiness. The arrangement was for the ransom of two million dollars to be paid into Archer's numbered account in a Swiss bank. On the face of it, that made sense, but what claim would he (Grenville) have on the money once it was in Archer's account? Suppose Archer disappeared?

Grenville began to sweat. Although a wastrel and a gigolo, he had an acute sense of self-preservation. How was he to safeguard himself against a possible con from Archer?

Lying in the semi-darkness, Grenville considered this problem.

*

At exactly 14.00, Max Segetti, with Jacques Belmont at the wheel of a battered VW, pulled up outside the Hotel de Suisse. Archer who had already checked out, was waiting for them in his rented Mercedes. He waved to them to follow him and drove through the busy streets of Lugano to the lake front and then on to Paradiso. He kept looking in his driving mirror to make sure the VW was following him.

After a ten-minute drive, he pulled up outside the rented villa. The VW parked by the Mercedes and Segetti and Belmont, carrying shabby suitcases, joined him. They were both wearing dark suits and looked slightly more respectable than when he had first seen them in Geneva.

'No problems?' Archer asked, speaking in Italian.

'No, sir,' Segetti said and smiled.

'You have the hoods and the guns?'

'Yes, sir. We came via Zurich to avoid the Italian customs. No problems.'

'Well, come in.' Archer led the way through the small neglected garden, unlocked the front door and entered the living-room. 'Sit down.'

The two men sat down in armchairs.

Archer began pacing the room.

'The operation will be at eleven o'clock tonight. You will find the front door of this villa unlocked. Burst in, threaten the man and the woman with your guns and take the man away. You will bring him here and that terminates our agreement. I will pay you, and you will leave immediately for Geneva and forget that it happened.'

Segetti nodded while Belmont sat motionless staring down at the threadbare carpet.

'And where is this villa, sir?' Segetti asked.

'I will take you there in a few minutes. There could be one difficulty. There is a manservant. He could be awkward. If he appears, one of you must take care of him.' Archer paused, then went on, 'There must be no violence.'

For the first time, Belmont spoke. With an evil little grin, he said, 'That's okay. I'll take care of him.'

The menacing note in his voice made Archer stare at him.

'I repeat ... no violence.' He looked at Segetti. 'Is that completely understood? I would rather the kidnapping failed than to have violence.'

'It won't be necessary, sir,' Segetti said.

'The man to be kidnapped will offer only a token resistance,' Archer went on, 'but nothing more. He wants to convince the woman that he is being kidnapped. You understand?'

'Yes, sir,' Segetti said.

'All right. Now I'll sum up: at exactly eleven o'clock tonight, you will arrive at the villa, using my car. You will park at the bottom of the drive. You will walk up the drive to the villa. The front door will be unlocked. You will burst in. The man and the woman will either be in the living-room or out on the terrace. As you enter the lobby, the door, leading to the living-room, will face you.' Archer took a sheet of paper from his wallet. 'Here is a plan of the villa. Look at it.'

Segetti studied the plan, then nodded.

'That is fine, sir,' he said.

Archer produced another slip of paper.

'I have written down the exact words you are to say to the woman and I want you to memorize these words.' He handed the slip of paper to Segetti. After reading the words, Segetti smiled. 'Jacques, this will be your job,' and he handed the paper to Belmont. Looking at Archer, he went on, 'Jacques can do this very well.'

'I don't care who says them so long as they are said convincingly,' Archer said. 'You will take the man to the car and drive him here. That's it. I will pay you, and you leave for Geneva immediately.'

'No problem, sir,' Segetti said.

'All right. I will now take you to the villa. Let's go.'

Archer, feeling more satisfied that these two men would do a successful job, drove them in his Mercedes to Castagnola. He drove slowly. From time to time, he asked Segetti, who was sitting at his side, if he could remember the route.

Segetti kept saying, 'No problem, sir.'

As Archer drove up the steep hill that led past Helga's villa, he slowed, but didn't stop.

'That's it. Villa Helios. I'll come back the same way.'

Both Segetti and Belmont peered at the wrought-iron gates that led to the villa as the Mercedes crawled by. At the top of the road, Archer reversed and then again drove slowly past the villa.

'Have you got it?' he asked.

'Sir, there is no problem.'

'All right. You have about eight hours. Do you want to stay at my villa or what do you want to do?'

'We would like to look at Lugano, sir,' Segetti said. 'We have never been here before. May I ask you to take us back so we can use our car?'

Archer was relieved. The thought of having these two with him for eight hours didn't appeal to him.

'Yes.'

He drove them back to the villa.

As they got out of the Mercedes, Segetti said, 'We will be here at 22.15 tonight, sir.'

Archer watched them drive away. He unlocked the door of the villa, went into one of the bedrooms and stretched out on the bed. He had a long wait, but at least, the operation was now in motion.

A million dollars! he thought. With that money he would go to New York. He would be able to start his own business as a tax consultant. There was nothing that bitch could do once he had her money. He was sure she would never cry 'thief'. She wouldn't want to face the blaze of publicity that she had been conned by a handsome gigolo as Herman Rolfe hadn't prosecuted because he knew Archer would have talked of his affair with Helga. No ... he had nothing to worry about as far as she was concerned. But these two men did worry him a little. There was something sinister about them, especially the young one. He would have been very worried if he had been able to see these two as they parked near the Lugano post office.

Leaving Belmont in the car, Segetti hurried into the post office and, shutting himself in a telephone booth, he called Bernie in Geneva. He talked briefly. Bernie listened, then said, 'Call me back in two hours, Max,' and he hung up.

Bernie had many contacts in Switzerland. One of his most reliable contacts was in Lugano: Lucky Bellini, so called because, many years ago, a jealous woman had plunged a knife into his fat back and he had survived.

'Lucky?' Bernie said. 'I want information. Who lives at a villa called Helios at Castagnola?'

'Helios?' Lucky's voice went up a note. 'That's the Herman Rolfe home. He's dead, but his wife uses it from time to time. She's there now.'

Bernie grinned.

'Stick around, Lucky,' he said. 'I'll be at your place sometime this evening,' and he hung up.

He called the airport and booked an air taxi that would get him to Agno, close to Lugano, at 18.00.

When Segetti called back, Bernie told him he would be joining him.

'Do just what this fink Archer tells you, Max. Collect this guy, then I'll handle it.'

'Sure, Bernie,' Segetti said. 'Where do we meet?'

'At the Agno airport at six o'clock. Pick me up there. Okay?'

'No problem, Bernie.'

Still smiling, Bernie hung up.

At midday, Grenville, not only bored to distraction, but also hungry, made his appearance on the terrace.

Helga was sitting at one of the big terrace tables, studying a file of papers. Seeing him, her face brightened.

'Dear Chris! Are you feeling better?'

Wearing a wan expression, Grenville crossed to her and kissed her lightly on her cheek.

'I'll survive.' He sank into a chair near hers. 'Do you think Hinkle could get me some coffee?'

'Of course, darling.' She rang the bell at the table. 'Are you really feeling better?'

'A bit shaken.' He gave her a brave smile. 'It's most odd. I haven't had an attack for months.'

Hinkle appeared.

'Coffee please, Hinkle. Mr. Grenville is feeling better.' Looking at Grenville, she went on, 'Wouldn't you like an omelette?'

Grenville, who would have preferred a steak, said he thought he could manage an omelette.

Inclining his head, Hinkle went away.

'I see you are working, Helga,' Grenville said. 'You carry on. I'll relax,' and leaning back, he closed his eyes.

After a moment's hesitation, Helga picked up the file.

When Hinkle brought the tray of coffee, toast and a herb omelette, Helga closed the file.

'Thank you,' Grenville said as Hinkle removed the silver cover to reveal the omelette. 'This looks marvellous.'

Hinkle inclined his head and walked away.

'We can talk business tomorrow,' Helga said. 'At last, Winborn is seeing sense. I had a long telephone call from him this morning. We are getting the site at our price.'

'Oh, good.' Grenville winced. 'Right now, darling, my brain feels scrambled. Do let's have a real discussion tomorrow,' he said, knowing there would be no tomorrow. He poured himself a cup of coffee.

'Of course.' Helga regarded him, then went on, 'You know, you are the very last person I would have thought was a migraine sufferer.'

'I inherited it from my father,' Grenville lied. 'He was a martyr to it.' He drank the coffee and poured another cup, then began to eat the omelette which he found excellent. 'Hinkle can certainly throw an omelette together.'

'Don't let him hear you say that,' Helga said uneasily. 'He creates omelettes, and, Chris dear, I want you to be really nice to him from now on. I must tell you, he doesn't approve of us getting married.'

Grenville stared at her, lifting his eyebrows.

'Doesn't approve? He's your servant, isn't he? Who cares if he approves or not? There are plenty of other servants.'

Helga stiffened, and the steely look came into her eyes.

'Chris, please. We must come to an understanding about Hinkle. There is no one, except you, who means so much to me. He has helped me so often in so many ways. He understands me. He . . .' She broke off and forced a smile. 'I don't want to sound dramatic about this, but Hinkle is part of my life, and I wouldn't lose him for all the money in the world!'

Grenville realized he had moved onto very dangerous ground, not that it mattered, but he didn't want to antagonize her.

Smiling, he said, 'Sorry. I didn't realize that he meant so much to you. I will do everything I can to make him approve of me. I promise you.'

'He does mean so much to me,' Helga said seriously. 'He is loyal and kind and utterly dependable.'

'I promise,' Grenville said and touched her hand.

'Thank you, Chris. I am sure he will come to know you as I know you and give you the same wonderful loyalty and service he gives me.'

God! Grenville thought. This drivel about a fat, pompous old butler! But he turned on his charm.

'I do hope he does.'

Just after 13.00, Hinkle appeared with a shaker of vodka martinis and two glasses. Grenville, remembering he was still supposed to be recovering from a severe attack of migraine, reluctantly refused, then turning to Hinkle, he went on, 'That was the most marvellous omelette! I can't imagine how you can make an omelette so light and delicious.'

'I am glad it pleased you, sir,' Hinkle said stiffly, then turning to Helga, 'For lunch, madame, I suggest a *mignon de veau* in a mushroom sauce and there is an excellent Brie to follow.'

'Wonderful.' Helga looked at Grenville. 'Do you feel like some?'

Grenville hesitated. The omelette hadn't taken the edge off his appetite.

'I think I could manage a little,' he said.

He felt Hinkle's disapproving eyes on him. When Hinkle had gone, Grenville said, 'He's not exactly loving me, is he?'

'You must give him time, darling.' Helga gathered up the papers. 'I have just time for a swim. You stay quiet,' and she went away.

Grenville longed for a swim, but that would be unwise. He counted the hours: only ten more! They would be dreary hours, but then he would be free! He lit a cigarette and relaxed back in his chair.

They lunched under sun umbrellas, then Helga insisted that Grenville should take a nap. He was willing enough and went to his own bedroom while she opened her file and reached for the telephone.

At 16.30, Grenville came out onto the terrace to find Helga still making notes and still studying the file.

'You never seem to stop working,' he said in dismay.

She smiled up at him.

'I am the head of a kingdom that is worth more than a billion dollars, Chris. You are going to be my strong right hand. When you own such a kingdom, it is very difficult to stop working. 'Ring for tea. I've just finished.'

To be married to this woman! Grenville thought. I would become a button on a calculator!

They spent the evening, talking. Helga eagerly made plans for their honeymoon. She had a yacht, she told him. Would he like to cruise around the Florida keys? Grenville agreed with all her suggestions, knowing thankfully that in a few more hours he would be free of her, plus a million dollars.

Watching her in the soft evening light, he felt a pang. She was really a beautiful woman, he thought. If only she wasn't so terrifyingly efficient, so frighteningly hard at times and so possessive. That steely look that came into her eyes and her voice when things weren't going her way scared him. No, he thought, I could never handle this woman to my advantage. The ball would always be in her court. Yet, he had regrets: she was marvellous in bed: she was lovely to look at and she was worth millions, but he knew she was too strong for him, and he knew, once married to her, she would completely dominate him. He wanted to be free, to have lots of money and to be able to pick up a dolly bird, use her, drop her and find a replacement. That was his idea of how to live: no complications and no more dreadful, fat old women. He looked furtively at his watch.

Hinkle came out on the terrace with the cocktail shaker and two glasses. This time, Grenville, who was longing for a drink, said he could manage a glass.

'I feel so much better, Hinkle,' he said with his most winning smile. 'Do you think I could have a steak?'

Helga, pleased, looked at Hinkle, but there was no benign expression on his face.

'Certainly, sir. A Tournedos Rossini or steak au poivre?'

You hostile sonofabitch, Grenville thought, but who cares? By tomorrow, I shall have forgotten you.

'A steak au poivre would be perfect.'

'Yes, Hinkle, for me, too,' Helga said. 'No starter. Could we have one of your champagne sorbets?'

As if to slight Grenville, Hinkle beamed at her.

'Certainly, madame,' and he went away.

Grenville sighed.

'I'm not making much of an impression, am I?'

'It'll take time,' Helga said. 'Be patient.'

'Of course.' He got to his feet. 'I'll change.'

After dinner, and when Hinkle had gone to fetch coffee, Grenville said, 'Shouldn't Hinkle relax now, Helga? He's not all that young, and he seems to have been on his feet all day.'

As Hinkle served the coffee, Helga said, 'That will be all, Hinkle. It was, as always, a lovely meal. Please leave us. We need nothing further.'

Hinkle inclined his head and picked up the tray.

'Very well, madame. I will retire. Mr. Grenville has only to lock the french windows and lower the shutters. The rest of the villa is secured.' He gave her a little bow. 'I trust you sleep well,' then, ignoring Grenville, he walked off the terrace.

Well, at least I've got rid of him, Grenville thought.

'There's a good movie on television,' he said. 'Shall we watch it?'

'Yes, but let's stay out here for a while. It's so lovely. What time does the film begin?'

'Nine forty-five.'

'Then we have time.' She put her hand on his. 'Are you sure you are feeling all right now, Chris?'

'I'm fine.' He smiled at her, 'After the film, I'll prove it.'

Her eyes sparkled.

'Darling! I'm so happy! You can't imagine what you mean to me!'

Grenville felt a tinge of conscience. In another hour and three-quarters! They could hear Hinkle clearing up in the kitchen. The moon's reflection on the lake, the mountains outlined against a star-filled sky and the scent of flowers made this a night for romance.

Later, Grenville, who was listening intently, heard Hinkle close the kitchen door and walk off to his room at the far end of the villa.

'Let's look at the film.'

They went into the living-room and Grenville turned on the TV set.

'I'll be back in a moment,' and he went out into the lobby, closing the living-room door. It took him only a few moments to draw the bolts, undo the safety chain and unlock the front door. Then he went into the toilet and flushed the cistern. He looked at his watch. Another hour!

He returned to Helga's side, his heart beginning to thump, and stared sightlessly at the lighted screen. All he could think of was that in an hour, an explosion would occur that would alter his whole way of life.

Fortunately, the film had a grip, and Helga was interested. She was completely relaxed, holding Grenville's hand, lying back in her chair, only one lamp to light the big room.

On the over-mantel was an illuminated clock, and Grenville kept looking at it.

As the hands of the clock moved to 23.00, the door jerked open and two men, wearing hoods, guns in hands, burst into the room.

109

CHAPTER SIX

ARCHER looked at his strap watch. The time was exactly 23.00. At this moment, he thought, Segetti and Belmont would be entering Helga's villa.

The two men had arrived at Archer's rented villa at 22.15 as arranged. They had shown him the two black leather hoods and two automatic pistols. Archer, who had served in the Army, knew about small arms and he examined both pistols, making sure they were unloaded. He again emphasized there was to be no violence.

'Rather than that drop the plan,' he said. 'You will be paid just the same. Do you understand?'

Segetti, grinning, said there would be no problem.

'And bring my friend back here. Don't speed. We don't want trouble with the police,' Archer went on.

When they had gone, he paced the small living-room, his eyes continually on his watch. If all went well, they should be back with Grenville by 23.30. If all went well . . .

Archer's suitcase was packed. He was ready for a quick take-off if something did go wrong. When dealing with a woman like Helga one just couldn't be sure. On the face of it, providing Grenville had really sunk a hook into her, she would pay up, but there was this steel in her that Archer had already encountered that made him wary of her.

He thought back to the time when he had tried to blackmail her and she had trapped him in a cellar of the Castagnola villa. Even when he thought he had had the last laugh on her, she had beaten him, and from that moment, he had become one of the shabby, fringe people, always scratching for money.

His face hardened. When Grenville arrived, and when he

had been assured the kidnapping had succeeded, Archer intended to call on Helga. It would be his moment of triumph, and he would take his revenge for what she had done to him.

Again he looked at his watch. 23.20. By now, if all had gone well, they would be on their way back. He thought of Hinkle. There could be a dangerous man! He had met him from time to time when Hinkle had been Herman Rolfe's personal servant, and he knew that Hinkle had disliked him, and that in spite of Hinkle's deceptive appearance he had as much steel in him as Helga had, and that was why Hinkle had come to admire Helga so much. They were two of a kind.

Was that the sound of a car approaching? Archer went quickly to the front door and opened it. The headlights of a car made pools on the road, but the car drove past. It was a warm evening, and the moon rode high. Breathing unevenly, Archer stood on the doorstep, waiting and listening. Several cars passed, then he saw the Mercedes. He drew in a sharp breath as the car pulled up outside the villa.

Grenville was the first to get out of the car. He came quickly up the path.

'All right?' Archer asked, a little breathlessly.

'Perfect.' Grenville laughed. 'Couldn't have been better!'

'Go inside. I'll take care of these two,' Archer said, suddenly feeling ten feet tall.

Segetti and Belmont came slowly up the path. Archer wanted to be rid of them. Hurriedly, he took six one thousand franc bills from his pocket.

'Any trouble?' he asked as Segetti approached.

'No, sir,' Segetti said. 'Jacques gave your message. The lady seemed impressed. No problem.'

'All right. Here's your money. Forget about this,' Archer said. 'Now get off to Geneva.'

Segetti paused to count the bills in the light of the moon, nodded, then said, 'Okay, sir. We'll go.'

Archer watched them climb into the VW and drive away, then going into the living-room, he found Grenville sitting in an armchair, smiling.

'It was a beautiful job,' Grenville said.

Archer opened a bottle of whisky he had bought on the way to the villa and poured drinks.

'Tell me about it.'

Grenville sipped his drink.

'I got rid of Hinkle around nine o'clock. Fortunately, there was a good film on television so I suggested Helga and I should watch it. While she was settling herself, I went out into the lobby and unlocked the front door. She thought I was taking a leak. At exactly eleven o'clock, just as the film was finishing, these two burst in. They were impressive.' Grenville laughed. 'For a moment, they startled me. You should have seen what they did to Helga. She flipped her lid. One of them told her it was a snatch and she would get a ransom note tomorrow. He was really very convincing. He had a voice that could cut up rusty iron. He just yelled at her ... frankly, he rather shook me. He was really very convincing.' Grenville laughed again. 'He said if she called the police, did anything until she was contacted, she wouldn't see me again. She just sat there turned to stone. I started protesting, but they shoved me around a little, and then, with a gun stuck in my back, they hustled me out. It was all over in five minutes.' He drew in a long, deep breath. 'Now I'm free! You know, Jack, she really was getting too much for me.'

'Never mind that,' Archer said sharply. 'Are you sure you really have a hook in her, Chris? This is vitally important. If you haven't, she could call the police.'

Neither of the men knew nor even suspected that as soon as the VW had rounded the bend in the road, Segetti had slammed on his brakes, and Belmont, acting on Bernie's orders, raced back to the rented villa. Moving like a shadow, he went around to the back door, forced the flimsy lock with a small jemmy he had with him, and moved, silently, into the kitchen. The door stood ajar and the living-room door was also ajar. He was in time to hear Grenville say, 'Hook in her? My dear chap, it's not a hook ... it's a harpoon. I wish you could have seen her when those two shoved me out of the

112

room. She looked stricken: old, faded. I really did a job on her,' and he laughed. 'Believe it or not, we spent a dreary evening discussing our honeymoon plans!'

'Good! Excellent!' Archer rubbed his hands. 'We are nearly home. Tomorrow, I will call on her. This is a meeting I have been dreaming of for many months. It will give me the greatest pleasure.'

'There's one thing I want to talk to you about, Jack,' Grenville said, after a pause. 'Two million dollars is a lot of money, and a lot of temptation.' He looked straight at Archer. 'The money is going to be paid into your Swiss account. What guarantee have I got that I shall get my share?'

Archer stared at him, shocked. Had he come so low that a worthless gigolo didn't trust him?

Angrily, he said, 'Of course you will get your share! We are in this together: fifty-fifty.'

'That's what you say,' Grenville returned, 'but how can I be certain, and I want to be certain.'

Archer hesitated. He was aware of his shabbiness. He was shrewd enough to understand he made a poor picture of a man who could be trusted.

'What do you suggest, as obviously, you don't trust me?' His voice was bitter.

'Don't take this personally, Jack. Frankly, I would never trust anyone when two million is concerned, and I don't suppose you would either. From now on, after you have seen her and arranged payment, we keep together,' Grenville said. 'I'll come with you to your bank and see you transfer my share to an account I will open with your people. Any objection?'

Archer shrugged.

'None at all. If that's what you want, I will arrange it.'

'That's what I want.'

'Consider it done,' Archer said. 'To raise the money, Helga will have to sell stock. I will give her three days, but not a day more. While we wait, we will stay here. You must keep out of sight, Chris. I have stocked the refrigerator, and although this place isn't a palace, it's not too bad.'

113

'I'll survive,' Grenville said and finished his whisky.

'Now there is a little matter I have to attend to.' Archer went to the sideboard and pulled open a drawer. From it, he took a polaroid camera. 'I bought this on my way up.'

'What's that for?' Grenville asked blankly.

'Manufacturing evidence,' Archer said, smiling. 'And here is another little item I bought,' and from the drawer he produced a bottle of tomato ketchup.

'Good God! Have you gone crazy?' Grenville exclaimed.

'Not at all, my dear Chris.' Still smiling broadly, Archer waved the bottle before Grenville. 'This little bottle of sauce is worth two million dollars.'

Belmont edged forward, moved into the lobby and peered into the living-room.

'It's a little messy, Chris,' Archer went on, 'but you must expect to make an effort for so much money. Let me dab some of this sauce on your face, then you will lie on the floor and I will take photographs. I assure you, when I show these photographs to Helga, she won't hesitate to pay up. I know Helga. She loathes any kind of violence.'

Grenville threw back his head and laughed.

'What a wonderful idea! Go ahead.'

Feeling he had heard enough, Belmont silently left the villa and raced back to the VW. As he scrambled in, Segetti sent the little car fast down the hill.

Lucky Bellini owned a small shop, specializing in all kinds of Italian goods, in a back street off the Piazza Grande, Lugano. He lived above the shop with his fat wife, Maria. His eight children, all earning good livings, had long left home, and Lucky missed them, for he was a family man. Before the last of them left, Lucky had built, at the end of a small plot of land behind his store, a warehouse, and above, a big room which he had furnished with a bed, a table and some armchairs and had installed a shower and a toilet. This was used by his son who had ambitions to be a drummer in a Pop group, and the sound of drums was something that drove Lucky crazy.

It was in this room that he and Bernie talked. Some fifteen years ago, Lucky was a Mafia Don in Naples. He was now seventy-four and had been glad to retire, but once a Don always a Don. He knew Bernie to have solid connections with the Naples people, and anything he could do for Bernie was all right with him.

'Tell me about this Rolfe woman,' Bernie said, glancing at his watch. The time was 23.00: Segetti and Belmont should be going into action. 'She interests me.'

Lucky, who always kept his ear to the ground, became informative. He said Helga Rolfe had inherited Rolfe's millions, and was now the top shot of the Rolfe Electronic Corporation. In her own right, she was worth around sixty to eighty million dollars, give or take. She had hot pants, and had it off from time to time with hotel waiters, barmen, and especially Italians.

'Since Rolfe died,' Lucky went on, 'she's quietened down as far as I know. She has now taken up with a fancy man who calls himself Christopher Grenville. They are staying together at the Helios villa.'

'Who is this fink?'

'Grenville? He's English, looks loaded, but that's probably a front. I've no information about him except I hear he has been living in Germany for some time.'

'Know anything about Jack Archer?' Bernie asked.

Lucky nodded.

'He used to look after Rolfe's money. He was once a big shot with a tax consultant firm in Lausanne and used to come here quite often when Rolfe lived at Helios. Then suddenly, he didn't come any more. I heard he got into trouble, dipping his fingers into Rolfe's money, but I don't know for sure. There was also talk he used to screw Rolfe's wife, but that could also be talk.'

Bernie considered this information, then nodded.

'Okay, Lucky. Go to bed. I'll be fine here.' He patted Lucky's shoulder. 'I've got a pot on the stove. When it comes to the boil, I'll see you get a cut.'

Lucky grinned.

'With all my kids, I need a little extra, Bernie. Stay here as long as you like. When you want something to eat — coffee, whisky, anything – use the telephone. I'll bring it to you.' He was under the impression that Bernie was in trouble with the police and needed a hide-out. Bernie, reading his thoughts, didn't disillusion him.

'Fine, Lucky. I could have a couple of friends here too. That be okay?'

'Everything is okay with you, Bernie, as long as they don't mind sleeping on the floor.'

'They won't.'

The two men shook hands, and Lucky descended the stairs and walked heavily back to his apartment. He told his wife that maybe Bernie was in trouble, and she would have to supply him with food. His wife, five years younger than her husband, threw up her hands, but didn't protest. For fifty years now, anything Lucky said to her had to be all right with her. She obeyed, and didn't ask questions.

Bernie lay on the truckle bed and thought. Just before midnight, Segetti and Belmont climbed the stairs and joined him. They gave him a blow-by-blow account of the kidnapping, and then Belmont went on to describe what he had heard at the rented villa between Archer and Grenville.

'They are taking this broad for two million dollars!' Belmont said, his little black eyes glistening. 'Imagine!'

Bernie sneered.

'They are amateurs. This broad is worth sixty million if not more. In Rome, the other day, our people ransomed some fink for seven million dollars. Now here's what we do . . .'

For the next half hour he talked, stabbing the air with a thick finger to emphasize every point he was making. When he had finished, he said, 'Get the idea?'

'*Mamma mia!*' Segetti exclaimed. 'What's our share, Bernie?'

'That we will discuss later,' Bernie said. 'There is some work to do yet. Now I am going to sleep. You two sleep on the floor,' and settling himself on the truckle bed, he closed his eyes.

Helga came slowly awake, and for some minutes, lay in a relaxed stupor. Then, when her hand reached for Grenville, groped and found nothing, she opened her eyes.

The sun was coming through the blinds. The bedside clock told her it was 10.00. Chris, she thought, was taking a swim, then the memory of the previous awful night struck her, and she sat up with a strangled scream. She found she was wearing only her bra and panties. She looked wildly around the room, seeing again those terrifying hooded monsters as they had burst in, guns in hand.

Her heart began to hammer and she had to clench her hands into fists to stop another scream.

There came a knock on the door, and Hinkle entered, pushing the coffee trolley 'I thought I heard you, madame,' he said gently, and going to her closet, he took out a wrap and draped it around her. 'I took the liberty to remove your dress last night. I thought you would rest more comfortably.'

She drew in a long, slow breath, and the steel in her exerted itself. She now remembered she had behaved very badly last night. She had completely lost control of herself. As soon as she heard the car drive Chris away, she had run screaming down the long corridor to Hinkle's room. He had been marvellous. She had clung to him, sobbing, and he had picked her up, speaking soothing words as if she were a child, and had carried her to her bedroom and laid her on the bed. Then he had sat by her side, holding her hand while she hysterically told him what had happened.

'I can't lose him! I must get him back!' she cried. 'Hinkle, what am I to do? I must . . .'

'You mustn't distress yourself. You must remember this happens so often these days. You must try to relax.'

'Hinkle! They could hurt him! I love him! I can't bear to think he is in the hands of those awful brutes!' She began to sob again. 'I couldn't live without him! He is my life now! He is everything I've ever longed for!'

'Madame Rolfe!' A sudden steely snap in Hinkle's voice startled her. 'You are being hysterical. I have told you: this has happened before. I will alert the police and . . .'

'No! No! No! You're not to go to the police! They said they would kill him if the police came into it! You don't know how vicious they sounded!'

'Then we must wait for the ransom demand,' Hinkle said. 'In the meantime, madame, kindly control yourself.'

But Helga was beyond control, and turning on her side, burying her face in the pillow, she sobbed her heart out.

Hinkle regarded her, disapprovingly, then he went into the bathroom, found her sleeping pills, mixed four in a glass of water, then returned to her. He pulled her around and held the glass to her lips.

'I don't want it! I don't want it!'

'Drink it, and stop acting like a child!' Hinkle barked.

She drank, shuddered and dropped back on her pillow.

'I love him so much,' she moaned. 'Pray God they don't hurt him.'

Holding her hand, Hinkle watched as the drug took effect. Still crying, still moaning, she drifted off into sleep.

Remembering how she had behaved, and how Hinkle had handled the situation, she looked shame-faced at him as he poured the coffee.

'You have been wonderful, Hinkle,' she said. 'I don't know what I would have done without your help, and I am ashamed I behaved so badly last night.'

'It is understandable, madame,' Hinkle said. 'In a few days, Mr. Grenville will be back with you, and you will be happy again.'

'I hope so!' She drank some of the coffee. 'They said the ransom demand would be today. Will they telephone?'

'That, I believe, madame, is the usual procedure. I will draw a bath for you. If there is a telephone call, I will take it.' He looked at her. 'And, madame, this could be a trying day for you. A woman faced with a difficult situation is always at her best when she is looking her best.'

He walked into the bathroom and turned on the mixer.

Helga bit back her tears. He is right, she thought. He is so loyal and kind! She waited until he had left the room, then she took a bath, worked on her face, put on a pale-blue silk shirt and black trousers and regarded herself.

I am Helga Rolfe, she told herself. I am in love! Chris will come back to me. I am one of the richest women in the world! I hold Herman Rolfe's magic key! I will buy Chris back no matter what it costs!

She walked out onto the terrace where Hinkle was watering the flowers. He regarded her and nodded his approval.

'If I may take the liberty, madame, you are very beautiful,' he said.

'Thank you, Hinkle, and you are so very kind.'

'There are a number of dead blossoms that need attention, madame,' Hinkle said. 'If I may suggest, you might care to attend to them. I find gardening very soothing, and we may have some time to wait.' He indicated secateurs and a basket near her and obediently, knowing he was trying to be helpful, Helga began to cut the dead flowers: something she had never done before. And, of course, Hinkle was right again. The task was soothing, but she continually thought of Grenville.

At 11.15, Hinkle appeared with a shaker and glass.

'I suggest a little refreshment, madame,' he said.

She nodded and went indoors, washed her hands, then returned to the terrace.

'Aren't they going to phone, Hinkle?'

'Yes, madame,' Hinkle said, as he poured the drink. 'You could call it a war of nerves, and I am confident that your nerves will remain steady.'

She sat down.

'It's only that I keep thinking they will hurt him. I can't bear the thought!'

'Why should they, madame?'

'They sounded so vicious.'

119

'It may be some time before they telephone. I suggest an omelette for lunch. You must keep up your strength.'

Then they heard the front door bell ring. Helga slopped her drink and turned white.

'Please, madame,' Hinkle said, completely unperturbed. 'It is probably the postman. I will see,' and he walked sedately across the terrace to the front door.

Opening it, he found himself face to face with Archer. The two men looked at each other, then Archer said jovially, 'How are you, Hinkle? You remember me?'

It said much for Hinkle's steel control that his expression didn't change. He lifted his eyebrows as he said, 'Mr. Archer, I believe.'

'That's right. I want to talk to Madame Rolfe.'

'Madame Rolfe is not at home,' Hinkle said stiffly.

'She'll see me. Tell her I am representing Mr. Grenville's interests.'

Hinkle stared for a long moment at Archer who continued to smile.

'If you will wait.' He paused to look Archer up and down, surveying his shabbiness, then he closed the front door, shooting the bolt.

Helga, tense, turned around, as Hinkle came onto the terrace.

She stiffened.

'Madame, Mr. Archer is calling,' he said.

'Who?'

'Mr. Jack Archer.'

Helga's eyes lit up with anger.

'Archer! How dare he come here! Get rid of him! I would never have that man in my house!'

'I suggest, madame, you should see him,' Hinkle said quietly. 'He said he ' was representing Mr. Grenville's interests.'

The shock made Helga close her eyes. The she pulled herself together.

'Is he behind this?'

'I don't know, madame, but it would appear so.'

The steel in Helga asserted itself. She stood up and walked into the living-room. Her mind flashed back to those few, but dreadful days, when Archer had been locked up in the cellar and had broken out, but she also remembered that she had beaten him, just when he had thought he had triumphed. She had known Archer for some twenty years. When she and he had worked in her father's firm, they had been lovers. It had been Archer who had persuaded her to marry Rolfe so that he could handle Rolfe's affairs in Switzerland. He had stolen two million dollars of Rolfe's money and had lost the money in a stupid speculation. He had tried to blackmail her not to tell Rolfe, but she had refused. She had beaten him that time: she could do it again, she told herself.

'Send him in, Hinkle. I will see him alone.'

'Very well, madame.'

As Hinkle passed the hi-fi set, he pressed a switch and a button.

Archer came bouncing in, smiling broadly.

'My dear Helga, how good to see you again!' he said in his booming voice. 'It is such a long time, isn't it?'

Hinkle quietly closed the door on them.

Helga, standing motionless, her head slightly back, gave him a steely stare. She looked him up and down, and then her lip curled.

'Ah! You see a change in me,' Archer said, still smiling. 'At the moment I am at low ebb, but the tide is rising.' He sat down, uninvited, and crossed one fat leg over the other. 'You still look most impressive, Helga. I really don't know how you do it at your age. But then, I suppose, money does make all the difference. Beauticians, hairdressers, massage, and of course, clothes.' He laughed. 'Even I could look impressive if I had some money, but you really did put me in a hole, Helga. You really did.'

'What do you want?' she said, steel in her voice.

'What do I want? Shall we say revenge? I remember so well – when was it? Ten months ago? When you said you held the four aces. Now it is my turn to hold four aces.' As she said nothing, but stood, waiting, he went on, 'I have often dreamed of this moment, Helga, when I would make you drink gall as you made me drink gall. Perhaps I should say vinegar,' and he laughed.

Although a brilliant international lawyer, Helga's father was given to old-fashioned clichés. So often he had said to her: *What you put in, you take out. Offence is better than defence.* They were clichés that remained in her mind. Once, when she had a difficult problem, he had said to her: *If you are in a tight corner, let the other man talk. Know your enemy. Listen hard enough, and you will find a weak spot.*

Know your enemy!

It was the soundest advice he had ever given her, and Helga remembered.

After a pause, Archer, smiling, said, 'Nothing to say?'

'I'm listening,' Helga said.

'Yes, you were always a good listener. You were always a good bluffer too, but this time, Helga, I hold the four aces.'

'Will you come to the point?' she said. 'I suppose it is money. You look shabby enough to need money.'

Archer flushed slightly. Before his theft, he had always prided himself on his appearance. He used to change his shirt twice a day, was always immaculate and paid a visit to the barber once a week. His enforced shabbiness was like a nagging toothache.

'Since you refused to help me in my trouble, life has been a little tiresome,' he said.

'Your trouble was that you became an embezzler, a forger and a blackmailer,' Helga said. 'You have only yourself to blame.'

'Not quite the way to talk to me,' Archer said, a sudden snarl in his voice. 'I . . .'

'But it is true, isn't it? Don't tell me you will deny that you are an embezzler, a forger and a blackmailer?' Helga said, lifting her eyebrows. 'Don't let me add liar as well.'

Feeling she was taking the initiative, Archer decided it was time to assert himself.

'I told your servant I was representing Mr. Grenville's interests.'

He saw her stiffen at the mention of Grenville's name, but she still was upright, and still had that steely look in her eyes.

'Well?'

'It is rather an odd story, Helga,' Archer said. 'Do sit down. It will take a little time, and I find it disturbing, seeing you standing there like the wraith of a goddess.'

Helga moved to a chair and sat down.

Archer glanced out on to the terrace.

'Ah, how nice! A shaker and a glass. Your usual vodka martini, I suspect. Actually Helga, I haven't had a vodka martini for many months. Excuse me.' He got up, crossed the terrace and poured the drink into Helga's unfinished glass. He drank, refilled the glass and carrying it back, settled in his chair again.

'Your servant still makes excellent vodka martinis. How lucky you are to be able to afford a servant.'

She sat still, her hands in her lap, her face expressionless. Inwardly, she was boiling with fury.

'As I was saying,' Archer went on, 'this is rather an odd story. Two days ago, I was approached by a man – obviously an Italian – who asked me if I would represent him for a fee of ten thousand francs.' Archer paused to sip his drink. 'Since you refused to help me over this little trouble with your husband's money I have found it difficult to make a living. It would seem your husband had me blackballed. Whenever I applied for work, I was turned down, so ten thousand francs was a godsend to me.' He smiled at her. 'There may possibly come a time when you might lose your money, although I think this is doubtful, but let me tell you, when you have no money, when you are forced to wear a suit like the one I have on, and don't know when you will be able to buy another, when you are forced to eat at some lowly bistro, and sometimes go without dinner, you will find your attitude towards what is right and what is wrong alters. So, when this man approached me, I listened. He told me you were living with Grenville, and that you appeared to be besotted with him. My client – I will call him that – has been watching both of you. He knows how rich you are. It seemed to him a good idea to kidnap Grenville and hold him to ransom, feeling confident you would want him back. My client is tough and vicious.' Archer paused, then went on, 'In fact, he made no secret that he is connected with the Mafia. Somehow, he learned that you and I were once close.' Archer smiled. 'And we were, weren't we, Helga? Let us say, we were very close.'

Helga remained motionless and listened but her hands turned into fists.

'He considered me – since I had this old association with you – to be the right man to negotiate the ransom. So here I am.'

'I will deal with this man direct, and not through you,' Helga said.

'You have no choice. My client wishes to remain in the background. If you want your fancy man back, Helga, you must deal with me. And besides, I need my client's fee.'

Helga regarded him with loathing.

'So you are not only an embezzler, a forger and a black-mailer, you are now a creature of the Mafia!'

Again Archer flushed.

'I will remind you, you are not in a position to be abusive,' he said, a snarl in his voice. 'You will pay two million dollars if you want Grenville back. My client is prepared to give you three days to collect the money which is to be paid into a Swiss bank. So, at this time in three days's time, I will call on you. It is up to you.' He finished his drink, set down the glass, then got to his feet. 'I need not remind you, when dealing with the Mafia you should be very, very careful. It would be quite lethal for Grenville, so my client tells me, if you contact the police.' He smiled. 'My client also said that if the money isn't paid within three days, you will receive one of Grenville's ears.'

Helga lost colour, but not her steel.

'It is a savage thing,' Archer went on, 'and it shocks me,

but that is the way the Mafia works. They are utterly ruthless people. Don't think this is an idle threat. It has been done before, if you recall the Getty affair. So I would advise you to look through your stock holdings and sell to your advantage – that is, of course, if you want Grenville back. I haven't met him, but if you have taken a fancy to him, knowing your taste, I assume he must be handsome. With an ear less, he could be less handsome.' As he made for the door, he paused. 'I was almost forgetting. My client gave me this sealed envelope. It is for you.' He put the envelope on the table. 'I hear Grenville tried to be brave: a mistake, when in the hands of the Mafia.' He paused, then went on, 'Well then, Helga, expect me in three days' time. 'Bye for now.' Leaving the villa, he got into the Mercedes and drove away.

Her heart hammering, Helga snatched up the envelope, tore it open, and took out three polaroid coloured prints. She took one horrified look at them, stifled a scream and dropped them on the floor as Hinkle came quietly into the room.

As Archer had anticipated, the photographs completely shattered Helga. She loathed violence. She could never watch any violent movie. Time and again, she had snapped off the TV set when someone was about to be shot or hurt. All the steel in her evaporated. She buried her head in her hands and began to sob wildly.

'They've hurt him! I knew they would! They've hurt him!' she moaned.

Hinkle gave her a disapproving look and picked up the photographs. He regarded them, pursed his lips, then putting them on the table, he touched her lightly on her shoulder.

'I suggest, madame, you should control yourself,' he said severely.

She stared up at him, her eyes wild.

'Look what they have done to him! They are fiends! I must get the money at once! I . . .' and she began to sob again.

Hinkle went over to the hi-fi set and snapped down the

125

switch. Then he went to a drawer, and from it, took a power-ful magnifying glass. Picking up the photographs, he exam-ined them carefully. At first glance, they were impressive, showing Grenville lying on the floor, blood on his face, his eyes closed. After studying the photographs under the mag-nifying glass for some moments, Hinkle nodded, and put them down on the table.

'Madame, if you can cease being hysterical,' he said, a snap in his voice, 'I wish to tell you something.'

Her face tear-stained, her body shaking, Helga looked up at him.

'Leave me alone! Go away!'

'Madame, I wish to tell you something.'

'What is it?'

Picking up one of the photographs, he waved it at her.

'This looks to me remarkably like tomato ketchup,' he said.

Helga was so astonished, she stopped crying.

'Tomato ketchup?' Her voice was husky and unsteady. 'Have you gone mad? What are you saying?'

'Before I entered Mr. Rolfe's service, madame, I had the misfortune to look after a gentleman in the movie business,' Hinkle said. 'From him, I learned the art of make-up. Ap-parently, tomato ketchup is used to simulate blood.'

'What are you trying to tell me?' The steel came back and her voice snapped.

Hinkle nodded his approval.

'I am suggesting, madame, that Mr. Grenville is not hurt. It would appear these photographs are fakes.'

Helga stiffened.

'You really think so, Hinkle? You don't think they have hurt him?'

'I think it is most unlikely, madame.'

'The devils!' she clenched her fists. 'But I must get him out of their hands. I . . .'

'Madame, I would like to ask you a question.'

'Oh, for God's sake, don't be so pompous!' she shrilled at him. 'I'm going out of my mind. What is it?'

Again Hinkle nodded his approval. This was Helga Rolfe as he knew her, not an hysterical weakling.

'How do you imagine these two men, who took Mr. Grenville away, got into the villa?' he asked.

'What the hell has that to do with it?' Helga snapped. 'They rushed in here and took him away!'

'But how did they get in?' Hinkle persisted.

She stared at him, then drew in a deep breath.

'Through the front door, of course.'

'I locked and bolted the front door, madame, before retiring.'

'You must have forgotten,' Helga said impatiently.

'Before retiring, madame,' Hinkle said quietly, 'I locked and bolted the front door.'

Helga looked at him, then nodded.

'I apologize. I'm worried out of my mind.'

'That is understandable. Nevertheless, these two men must have come in by way of the front door. Did Mr. Grenville leave you to go to the lobby toilet?'

Helga's eyes opened wide.

'Yes, but . . .'

'Then I suggest Mr. Grenville unlocked and unbolted the front door. There could be no one else.'

'Are you daring to suggest that Mr. Grenville engineered his own kidnapping?' Helga shrilled.

'These photographs are fakes, madame. Mr. Grenville was the only one here who could unlock the front door,' Hinkle said. 'The conclusion is obvious.'

'No! He loves me! He would never, never do such a thing!' Helga began to beat her fists together. 'I won't listen to you! I know you hate him, but I love him! I won't listen to you!'

'Before leaving you with Mr. Archer, I took the liberty of turning on the tape recorder,' Hinkle said, unperturbed. 'We have a recording of the conversation between you and Mr. Archer. I have also the number of his car. I suggest, madame, we should now seek the help of the police.'

'The police? No! Chris is in the hands of the Mafia! They are threatening to cut off his ear unless I pay.' Jumping to her feet, she stared wildly at him. 'What is money? I don't give a damn as long as I get him back! I'll pay! I'm not listening to your insinuations! You are suggesting hateful things because you hate him! Keep out of this! I am going to get him back, no matter what it costs!' She ran from the room and into her bedroom, slamming the door.

For a long moment, Hinkle stood still, his face clouded, then he moved out onto the terrace. He stood by the terrace rail, staring out across the lake, his mind busy.

Archer eased his heavy body in the driving seat of the Mercedes as he drove through Cassarate and headed towards the lake road to Paradiso.

He was feeling relaxed and satisfied. He had certainly dug the knife into that bitch and had turned the blade. He chuckled. It was a pity he hadn't seen her reaction when she had looked at those photographs, but he could well imagine how she would have gone to pieces. To see her darling lover with blood on his face would utterly demoralize her. He was sure he would have no trouble with her. She would pay up.

A million dollars! he thought. In three days' time, he would be able to buy himself as many suits as he wanted. He could go to the barber once a week instead of cutting his own hair. He could once again eat at the best restaurants; stay at the best hotels! she deserved no pity. She had given him none in the past. This was sweet revenge!

It had been a brilliant idea of his to let her imagine Grenville was in the hands of the Mafia. How Grenville would laugh. Damn it! They must celebrate. Then he frowned. Grenville must keep out of sight until the money was paid, but at least they could have a bottle of champagne. Archer nodded. Yes, he thought, splendid idea – an idea Grenville would appreciate.

After some difficulty, he found parking in Lugano, and went to the Inno store. There, he bought two bottles of good champagne, then selected a variety of hors d'oeuvres with several cheeses. They would have a little feast, while he told Grenville how clever he had been.

Carrying his purchases, he returned to the Mercedes and

headed back to his rented villa. By now, he thought, Helga would be busy examining her list of stock holdings, trying to make up her mind which to sell. Whatever stock she did sell to make up two million dollars, she would be the loser. The Dow Jones index was flat on its back. Serve the bitch right! That was her funeral, and Archer laughed. He could imagine her driving her fancy Rolls to Bern to consult her banker, panic gnawing at her. Sweet revenge!

The four aces, he thought. I hold them all, and this time, she can't bluff her way out! I have her exactly where I want her!

He pulled up outside the rented villa, collected his purchases and hurried up the path. He opened the front door.

'Chris! It worked!' he shouted.

Silence greeted him.

Frowning, he walked into the empty living-room, then into the bedroom, then into the second bedroom. There was no sign of Grenville. Suddenly uneasy, Archer looked into the kitchen, hurried to the bathroom and threw open the door to the toilet.

Grenville was not in the villa.

CHAPTER SEVEN

GRENVILLE had watched Archer drive away, then he had returned to the shabby little living-room and had sat down. He would probably have an hour to wait before Archer returned. He didn't envy Archer. He had now learned that Helga could be all steel, but Archer had seemed very confident. Grenville had no doubts that she was madly in love with him. He just hoped that Archer would handle her carefully. He was now satisfied that he could trust Archer. All the same, he told himself, he would keep close to Archer, once the money was paid. When such a sum was involved, one couldn't be too careful.

He lit a cigarette, as he followed in his mind Archer's progress through Cassarate and up to Castagnola. He looked at his watch. In another ten minutes, he thought, Archer would be arriving at Helga's villa. It was a bore that they had to stay in this miserable little villa for three days, but he bowed to Archer's warning that he must not show himself on the streets. It would be a complete give-away if he were spotted. The Swiss police were busy-bodies, Archer had said, and they always looked twice at foreigners. He remembered the policeman who had threatened to give him a parking ticket. He frowned. He had behaved stupidly. That policeman had his name and address and would recognize him again. Thinking about the incident, Grenville shrugged his shoulders. It didn't matter, he told himself. In three days' time, he would be at the Geneva airport, waiting to take-off for New York, then from New York, he would fly down to Miami, spend a couple of days there, and then on to the West Indies.

He wondered what Archer would do with his share of the

money. Thinking about Archer, Grenville decided he wasn't a bad fellow, and, there was no doubt, he had brains. Given decent clothes, Grenville thought, and a respectable haircut, he could look quite impressive. Thank God, he told himself, that he had never got so financially low as Archer had. There had always been some stupid woman to finance him, but with a million dollars, he would be free of all that, and he would be independent!

A slight sound behind him made him look around.

Standing in the doorway was Segetti, and just behind him, Belmont. Startled, Grenville jumped to his feet.

'What are you two doing here?' he demanded sharply. 'I thought you were on your way to Geneva.'

'We changed our minds,' Segetti said, and moved into the room. 'Didn't we, Jacques?'

Belmont didn't say anything. He leaned against the door-post and stared bleakly at Grenville.

'So what do you want?' These two looked unpleasantly menacing and Grenville had a presentiment of danger. He moved away from the armchair in which he had been sitting.

'What do we want?' Segetti smiled. 'We want you, Mr. Grenville.'

'What do you mean?' Grenville's heart began to thump.

'You understand English? We want you to come with us.'

'That's the last thing I'll do,' Grenville blustered. 'Now stop this nonsense. You have been well paid. Get out!'

'This time, Mr. Grenville, it won't be tomato ketchup, it will be for real,' and Segetti produced a vicious-looking Luger automatic, fitted with a silencer. He pointed the gun at Grenville.

Grenville felt a rush of cold blood up his spine. Never before in his life had anyone threatened him with a gun. The sight of that evil-looking little hole in the silencer directed at him, brought him out in a sweat of fear.

'Don't point that thing at me!' he quavered. 'Don't – don't shoot!'

'Come along, Mr. Grenville,' Segetti said. 'We are going

for a little drive. You will sit in the front seat. I shall be in the back seat. If you attempt to do anything foolish, you will get a silent bullet through your spine.' He smiled. 'I don't make idle threats. Let's go.'

Shaken, his mouth dry, sweat on his face, Grenville followed Belmont down the path to the parked VW. Segetti, pointing the gun at him, slid into the back seat, motioning Grenville to get in the front seat. Belmont slid under the driving wheel.

'Where are you taking me?' Grenville asked huskily. 'What do you want with me?'

'Just keep your trap shut, Mr. Grenville, and you'll be fine.'

They drove along the lake road, passed a policeman who was directing a pedestrian, asking the way, and Grenville looked longingly at the policeman, but Segetti said softly, 'No foolish ideas, Mr. Grenville.'

Entering the Piazza Grande, they turned up a side street, and Belmont pulled up.

'Be careful how you get out, Mr. Grenville,' Segetti said, 'I am a very good shot.'

For a moment, Grenville, who was now in a panic, asked himself whether, as soon as he was out of the car, he should make a dash to escape, but the street was deserted, and he hadn't the nerve. He got out, followed by Segetti.

Belmont pushed open a high wooden gate and jerked his head at Grenville, who followed him through the gateway into the untidy yard. Segetti followed.

Ahead of him, Grenville saw a big building, like a barn, and he followed Belmont into the semi-darkness of the place which smelt strongly of cheeses, olive oil and anchovies. Belmont climbed steep stairs. Segetti prodded Grenville up the stairs and into a big room in which stood a bed, a table, several battered armchairs and a radio. Sitting in one of the chairs was Bernie.

'Ah, Mr. Grenville,' he said, getting to his feet. 'We haven't met before, but we have a mutual friend – Mr. Archer.'

Grenville regarded this short, squat, bearded Italian the way he would have regarded a big, hairy-legged spider that had dropped into his bath. In spite of Bernie's smile, his small eyes, like two sea-washed pebbles, chilled Grenville.

'You know Archer?' Grenville's voice was husky.

'Of course. Come in, Mr. Grenville, and sit down. I want to talk to you.'

Moving shakily, Grenville sank into an armchair, aware that Segetti was just behind him, and Belmont was leaning against the door.

'I don't understand,' Grenville said. 'What do you want with me?'

'Let me explain,' Bernie said, resuming his chair. 'Mr. Archer came to me, saying he wanted to hire two reliable men for a faked kidnapping. Mr. Archer explained the kidnapping was a joke, and, frankly Mr. Grenville, I didn't believe this. It seemed to me that his offer to me of five hundred francs to find two men, and his offer to pay these two men eight thousand francs for a job that could get us all into police trouble was inadequate.' He smiled. 'Now I discover that he and you intend to get two million dollars from this woman, so naturally, since, without my help, this kidnapping couldn't have been accomplished, I feel our share should be considerably increased.'

'You should have discussed this with Archer,' Grenville said, trying to steady his voice. 'Why bring me here by force?'

'That is a good point,' Bernie said. 'Why bring you here by force? Because you have now been kidnapped, and this kidnapping is no fake.'

Grenville drew in a sharp breath.

'I still don't understand,' he managed to say.

'Mr. Grenville, you and Mr. Archer are amateurs. Here you have a situation involving a woman worth about eighty million dollars. You have said that you have a harpoon in her.' Bernie looked at Belmont. 'That was what he said, Jacques?'

Belmont nodded.

'So ...' Bernie lifted his hands 'The woman is obviously besotted with you. Accept my congratulations, but when a woman is worth some eighty million dollars, no one, but an amateur, would ask two million to get her stud back. Do you see my point?'

Grenville ran his tongue over his dry lips.

'She – she's difficult,' he said huskily. 'I think two million is enough.'

'But then you and Mr. Archer are amateurs. From now on, Mr. Grenville, I intend to handle this affair. Only the other week, an industrialist was kidnapped in Rome by a good friend of mine, and the ransom demand was seven million dollars, and this industrialist wasn't nearly as rich as this woman, and yet to save his skin, he paid up.' Bernie leaned forward, pointing a stubby finger at Grenville. 'I will ask ten million dollars for your return, Mr. Grenville. For your co-operation, I will give you five hundred thousand dollars, and I will give Mr. Archer the same amount.'

Grenville stared at him.

'Co-operation? What does that mean?'

'You might be asked to lose an ear or a finger, Mr. Grenville, but for five hundred thousand dollars, that isn't much to ask.'

Grenville's face expressed horror.

'You can't do that to me!'

'Mr. Grenville, you haven't as yet realized you have been kidnapped and this time, it is no fake. Jacques can slice off your ear and heal the wound with a hot iron without any trouble. He can also remove one of your fingers without you suffering too much. That is no problem, and from what I hear about your relations with this woman, she will pay.'

Grenville felt faint. He leaned back in the chair, sweat running down his face.

Bernie got to his feet.

'I am now going to talk to Mr. Archer. I shall want him to act as my go-between. It is safer that way. Just relax, Mr. Grenville. It is very possible you won't lose an ear or a finger. Max and Jacques will look after you.' He turned to Segetti.

'In half an hour, Max ... as we arranged,' and leaving Grenville, shuddering, his face in his hands, Bernie left the room.

Helga paced up and down in her bedroom. She was distraught. Chris! Kidnapped! In the hands of Mafia thugs! All she could think of was to get him back unharmed. What he must be suffering! She must get the money as quickly as possible! There must be no hitch! When that swine Archer came, she must have the money ready to give him!

She would drive to Bern immediately and see her Swiss banker. He must arrange to have the money transferred to the Mafia immediately!

Then realizing she was in an utter panic, she pulled herself together, and some of her steel asserted itself. She sat down, her fists clenched between her knees.

Hinkle!

He had actually dared to insinuate that Chris had engineered his own kidnapping! Hinkle was a jealous old fool! The moment she had told him she was in love with Chris, he hadn't been able to conceal his disapproval. When she had told him that she and Chris were going to be married, his congratulations and best wishes had been sour, and she knew why: he hated the idea of having a master again as well as a mistress. He was so goddamn selfish, he didn't want her to be happy, because it didn't suit him! He wanted her to live her lonely, loverless life, so he could fuss over her, providing her with his goddamn omelettes, while she ached and ached for a lover like Chris!

Tomato ketchup!

That had been a vicious lie! She was sure Grenville had been struck down! Hadn't that swine Archer said that Grenville had tried to be brave? She could imagine Chris in the hands of those thugs. He could have found an opportunity to attack them. Yes! She could imagine him – her splendid Chris – making a fight of it. She shuddered, thinking again of those pictures, showing him lying on the floor, blood on his face.

Tomato ketchup!

That proved the extent of Hinkle's possessive jealousy.

The unlocked front door?

Of course there was an explanation for that! Again, Hinkle had tried to undermine her faith in Chris.

What was more natural for Chris to unlock the door to stand for a moment on the doorstep to look at the night sky and the stars and to breathe the night air? Why should he have bothered to relock the door?

The steel in her asserted itself, and she got to her feet. She would go immediately to Bern!

She snatched up her handbag, took a light dust-coat from the closet and walked into the living-room.

Hearing her, Hinkle came to the door of the terrace.

'I am going to Bern,' she said curtly. 'I must arrange this ransom. I will be back some time this evening.'

'Madame, may I suggest ...' Hinkle began, but she cut him short.

'You may suggest nothing! I am shocked by your insinuations about Mr. Grenville! I will not tolerate such a narrow-minded attitude, although I understand why you have taken this attitude. I intend to marry Mr. Grenville when I get him back! You will either serve Mr. Grenville and myself or you must leave! Is that understood?'

Hinkle stiffened, then looked directly at her. There was such a sad, shocked expression in his eyes that shame swept over her.

'You are at liberty, madame, to do as you wish,' he said quietly.

Furious with herself for feeling shame, Helga shrilled, 'And I will do as I wish!' She walked fast from the room, jerked open the front door and ran down the steps to the garage.

For a long moment, Hinkle stood motionless, then as he saw the Rolls drive away, he closed the front door and locked it.

He returned to the living-room. For some minutes he moved around the room, his face clouded, then abruptly, as if his mind was made up, he went along the long corridor to his own quarters. In his bedroom, he hunted for and found a leather-covered address book. He thumbed back the index F and found the name he wanted: Jean Faucon.

Reaching for his telephone, he dialled a Paris number.

Archer sat slumped in an armchair, staring bleakly around the shabby little living-room.

Where was Grenville?

Surely, Archer asked himself, Grenville couldn't have been so reckless as to leave the villa and show himself on the streets? No! After Archer's repeated warnings that Grenville must remain in the villa until the ransom was paid, he was sure Grenville hadn't wandered out for a walk. Then what had happened to him? Why had he vanished? Where was he?

Archer thumped his fat knees with his fists. Just when it looked so good! He was certain Helga would pay! And now, Grenville had vanished!

Then a thought occurred to him. It could be that Grenville had lost his nerve, and as soon as Archer had driven away, he had left the villa, walked down to the bus stop and was already on a train, taking him from Switzerland! That could be the only explanation! This handsome, useless gigolo had lost his nerve and had bolted!

A surge of bitterness ran through Archer. It was all right for Grenville. He was still reasonably young, handsome, and with this sexual attraction which elderly women couldn't resist. He could always find some stupid, rich woman who would keep him. He wouldn't get a million dollars from her, but at least, he would be able to live in luxury.

Archer closed his eyes as he thought of his own future: back again to the shabby, fringe people with their hopeless plans to make millions, to float impossible loans, to sell land that they didn't own, with him accepting miserable fees to do their legal work. That was his future, getting shabbier and shabbier, continually hunting for money on which to live. He thought of Joe Patterson. There was no hope of returning to him. He would now have to find another client, but not in Switzerland. Perhaps in England. He still had ten thousand francs in his Swiss account, but if he drew on that, he would have nothing left.

Grenville had seemed so sure of Helga. What could have happened to make him change his mind and bolt?

Damn him! Archer thought. Damn him!

There was now no point in remaining in this shabby little villa. Grenville was gone. The sooner he left Lugano and was on his way to England, the better. As he got to his feet, the front door bell rang.

Archer stiffened and his heart skipped a beat. Who could it be? Had Helga alerted the police? He thought that was unlikely, but he could never be sure of Helga's reactions. Was this the police? He hesitated, then as the bell rang again, he forced himself to go to the front door and open it.

The shock of seeing Bernie, smiling, standing on the doorstep, made Archer's heart skip again.

'Ah, Mr. Archer,' Bernie said. 'So nice to see you again. How are you?'

Immediately Archer's shrewd, quick brain clicked into action. This short, squat, bearded Italian with his oily smile and menacing eyes must be the explanation of Grenville's disappearance.

He forced a smile as he stood back.

'This is a surprise, Bernie,' he said. 'What are you doing here?'

Bernie, still smiling, moved forward while Archer gave ground. Bernie stepped into the lobby.

'We have affairs to discuss, Mr. Archer,' he said.

'Come in.' Archer led the way into the living-room. 'What is it?'

Bernie looked around, then selecting a chair, he sat down.

'Mr. Grenville has been kidnapped,' he said.

As soon as he had seen Bernie standing on the doorstep, Archer knew he was in for trouble, but this statement shook him.

'Kidnapped? By whom?'

'By me.' Bernie smiled. 'Mr. Archer, you are an amateur.

Your faked kidnapping was stupid. I have taken over the operation. To get Grenville back, this Rolfe woman will have to pay ten million dollars. I am prepared to pay you and Grenville five hundred thousand dollars each to co-operate, but the rest of the money comes to me. You are to be my go-between. You will tell this woman the ransom has been increased from two to ten million.'

'Ten million!' Archer gasped. 'She won't pay!'

'She will when she gets one of Grenville's ears which you will deliver to her.'

Archer's legs suddenly felt boneless and he dropped into an armchair.

'Mr. Archer, this is now no longer a game,' Bernie said. 'I have Grenville, and I am quite prepared to send her his ear, and if she even hesitates, I will send her one of his fingers. I mean business, Mr. Archer, not like your childish bluff with tomato ketchup.'

Archer shuddered, then he pulled himself together.

'You must handle this yourself,' he said. 'I am leaving immediately. I will have nothing further to do with it!'

Bernie laughed.

'Mr. Archer, you will do what I tell you.' He produced from under his coat the silenced Luger. 'I assure you, I will shoot you if you don't co-operate. This gun makes no noise. You will be found here after some time, dead and rather smelly, and the police will have no idea who shot you. So you will co-operate.'

Archer stared with horror at the menacing gun.

'Yes ... all right,' he said, his voice husky. 'Yes, I will do what you say.'

Bernie nodded and put away the gun.

'Sensible man.' He paused, then went on, 'I understand you have given this woman three days to collect the two million dollars. That is all right. It is good for her to sweat. On the third day, you will go to her and tell her she must now find ten million dollars in two days. Unless she does, you will give her one of Grenville's ears.'

At this moment, the telephone bell began to ring.

Bernie waved to the telephone.

'Answer it, Mr. Archer.'

Moving unsteadily, Archer got out of his chair and picked up the receiver.

As soon as he said, 'Hello,' Grenville's hysterical voice exploded over the line.

'Jack! I've been kidnapped! This is your fault! These men are vicious! You've got to do something! I should never have listened to you! You've got to get me free! They are threatening to cut my ear off! I . . .' There was a click and the line went dead.

Shaken, Archer replaced the receiver.

'That was Mr. Grenville,' Bernie said. 'I arranged the call so you wouldn't think I was bluffing. Now listen to me, Mr. Archer, the day after tomorrow, you will go to this woman and tell her she is to pay ten million dollars in bearer bonds if she wants her lover back. I will leave it to you to be convincing, and for Mr. Grenville's sake, you had better be convincing!' Again he smiled. 'If I were in your place, Mr. Archer, under this pressure, my thinking would be that my amateur plan had gone sour. I would then think only of myself, and I wouldn't be bothered about Mr. Grenville. I would decide my best plan would be to leave Switzerland and forget the whole thing.' Bernie grinned evilly. 'But that would be wrong thinking. I am not an amateur. I have an organization here. From now on, you will be watched. If you attempt to run away, you will meet with a fatal accident. I don't want you dead, Mr. Archer, so I want your passport, just in case you are ready to take the risk and run.' He held out his hand.

'Give it to me!'

Slowly and reluctantly, Archer took out his passport and gave it to Bernie.

'Now we are organized,' Bernie said, getting to his feet. 'Then the day after tomorrow, you will see this woman and arrange the affair. Make it convincing, Mr. Archer. You understand?'

Archer nodded.

'That is good. 'Bye now: you will be seeing me.'

Bernie left the villa and, walking down the path, he got into the VW.

His heart pounding, his face ashen, Archer watched him drive away.

On the long, slow drive to Bern, Helga, behind the wheel of the Rolls, was haunted by the sad, shocked expression in Hinkle's eyes. She tried to steel herself. She told herself she could not allow herself to be controlled by this man, although, she knew, without him, there would be an irreplaceable hollow in her life. She was furiously ashamed of herself for having spoken to him as she had done. Suppose he took her seriously? Suppose he did leave her? It was unthinkable! But Chris now was her life! If she had to choose between Chris and Hinkle, she knew whom she would choose. And yet, life without Hinkle . . .

She was half out of her mind with worry when she sat down in the Director's office in the bank.

The Director, slim, youngish with a Swiss reserve, had an efficiency that gave her confidence.

'I need two million dollars in cash,' she said. 'I want it by tomorrow.'

'Certainly, Madame Rolfe. I have studied your portfolio. It is an unfortunate time to sell. To raise two million by selling some of your shares would mean a twenty-five per cent loss. I suggest we lend you the money. The bank charge would be eight-and-a-half per cent. That, I suggest, would be a better way.'

'Would you lend me the money?'

'But, of course.'

'The money is to be transferred to a numbered account,' Helga said. 'I will give you the number and the name of the bank later.'

'There is no problem, Madame Rolfe.'

Ten minutes later, Helga was driving back to Lugano. The time now was 16.00. She still felt so bad about Hinkle she couldn't face spending the rest of the evening at the villa.

She stopped at the Eden Hotel and drank a vodka martini on the terrace. She then walked along the lakeside, her mind continually on Grenville, and then on Hinkle.

Around 19.00 she realized she hadn't eaten all day, so she walked to her favourite restaurant, Bianchi, on via Pessina.

Dino, one of the head-waiters, who always looked after her, welcomed her.

'Madame Rolfe! This is a great pleasure!'

Seated, she asked what she could eat.

'Something light, Dino.'

'Then I suggest Puccini toast and a poussin in mushroom sauce.'

She nodded.

While she ate, her thoughts turn to Hinkle. She must win him over! She must convince him that Chris was now part of her life, and she couldn't live without him. She must convince Hinkle! She must win him over!

She returned to the villa a little after 20.00. As she drove into the garage, she saw the lights were on, and as she climbed the steps to the front door, it opened.

Hinkle stood in the doorway, his fat face expressionless and he gave her a stiff little bow.

'I have arranged everything,' she said, moving by him and going into the living-room.

After closing and locking the front door, Hinkle joined her.

'Will you require dinner, madame?'

'No, thank you. I had dinner in Lugano.' She dropped into a chair. 'Hinkle, I want to talk to you.'

'Certainly, madame.' He moved farther into the room, but away from her.

'I am a woman in love, Hinkle. When a woman loves as I do, she is unreasonable, stupid and hurtful. Chris is my life! I want you to understand. I am asking you to forget what I said to you this morning. You are part of me, Hinkle! Without you, I would be lost.' Tears filled her eyes. 'I am so worried and unhappy, but that doesn't excuse me. I am very, very sorry to have spoken to you as I did. Will you please be kind and forgive me? Will you please understand?'

Obviously moved, Hinkle said, 'As long as you need me, madame, I shall be happy to serve you. While we are speaking frankly, I would also like to say that I have great admiration for you. Ever since you married Mr. Rolfe, I have learned from experience that you are a remarkable lady. You have something I always admire ... courage.' He paused, then looked directly at her, 'And, madame, you will need your courage.' With a little bow, he went on, 'If you will excuse me, there are things I have to attend to,' and he left her.

Feeling utterly alone, Helga walked out onto the terrace and stared at the moon-lit lake. She thought of Chris. The night and the next day stretched interminably before her.

Courage?

What did Hinkle mean?

That night she took three sleeping pills and was mercifully released from her thoughts.

At 08.30, Hinkle tapped on her door and wheeled the coffee trolley into her bedroom. A little drowsy from her sleeping pills, Helga lifted herself off the pillow.

'Punctual as usual, Hinkle,' she said, smiling at him. 'I'm longing for coffee.'

'I trust you slept well, madame,' Hinkle said as he poured the coffee.

'I took three sleeping pills.'

He handed her a cup of coffee and then stood back.

'Madame, this is going to be a trying day for you. I understand Mr. Archer won't be calling until tomorrow morning.'

Helga nodded.

'I suggest then that you should seek distraction. Time hangs heavily when you have nothing to do but wait.'

'I'll be all right,' Helga said. 'I will sit on the terrace. I have things to think about.'

'That is the worst thing you could do, madame,' Hinkle said firmly. 'I suggest a visit to Como to look at the shops and have lunch there. Sitting on the terrace will only increase the tension.'

He was right, of course. She had a bleak thirty-six hours to wait before Archer arrived. During those hours, there was nothing she could do to help Chris.

'All right, Hinkle. I'll go to Como.'

She wasn't to know that Hinkle was anxiously awaiting a telephone call from Jean Faucon, and he didn't want Helga to be in the villa when the call came.

Her face drawn and white, Helga finally drove away at 11.00, and Hinkle sighed with relief. He paced uneasily up and down the terrace, every now and then, looking at his watch.

The anxiously awaited telephone call didn't come until 13.30. Hinkle had done the housework and had given himself a sandwich lunch. When he heard the telephone bell ring, he half ran into the living-room and snatched up the receiver.

Helga fought her way through the heavy Como traffic, and finally, found parking for the Rolls. She wandered around the town, staring sightlessly at the shop windows, her thoughts on Chris. What was he doing at this moment? Were those awful thugs giving him anything to eat? The money would be ready tomorrow, and when that swine Archer came, she would give it to him, and by the evening, Chris would be back with her! She felt a surge of sexual excitement run through her as she thought of tomorrow night. He and she together again! What was two million! Nothing to her! She loved him ... God! how she loved him! As soon as she got him back, they would fly to Paradise City, and they would get married. She now felt confident that she had made her peace with Hinkle. Villa Helios must be sold. It now had too many painful memories. She could never live there again. After lunch, she drove back to Lugano, and seeing an estate agent's sign, and for something to pass the time, she parked the Rolls and went into the agent's office. She talked to a smooth-looking Swiss who said he would be able to sell the villa without trouble. He had a rich client who was looking for just such a place and her asking price was reasonable. Without regret, she told him she would give vacant possession in two weeks.

Feeling more relaxed, she had a grilled steak at the Eden Hotel, then drove back to the villa.

As she was approaching the entrance to the villa, she was surprised to see a policeman in brown uniform on a motor-cycle come down the drive. He swept by her, his white helmet glittering in the moonlight.

She garaged the car, and then walked up the steps as Hinkle opened the front door.

'What was that policeman doing here?' she asked sharply.

Hinkle's face was expressionless as he said, 'I forgot to register at the Commune, madame. It is now in order. Did you have a satisfactory day?'

'All right.' She walked into the living-room. 'I have put the villa on the market. As soon as Mr. Grenville has returned, we will leave for Paradise City. I want you to stay on here, to get rid of the furniture, and to see the sale through. Will you do that?'

'Certainly, madame.'

She smiled at him.

'You are so reliable, Hinkle. Once this place is sold, I want you to come back and arrange everything for the wedding.'

'I am at your service, madame.' There was a sad look in Hinkle's eyes that disturbed her.

'It will be all right, won't it, Hinkle?'

'Let us hope so, madame. Is there anything I can get you?'

She looked at the clock on the over-mantel. It was now at 21.15. She had fourteen more hours to wait before Archer arrived.

'No. I'll go to bed.' She looked at him. 'Be patient with me, Hinkle. I keep thinking of him .. what he is doing .. how those awful people are treating him.'

'I understand, madame.'

She put her hand on his arm.

'I don't know what I would do without you, Hinkle.'

Leaving him, she went into her bedroom and closed the door. Hinkle locked up, secured the shutters, and then went to his quarters. On his bed lay a bulky envelope that the policeman had delivered.

Putting on his glasses, and tearing open the envelope, Hinkle sat down to read what Jean Faucon had sent him.

Helga was awake when Hinkle wheeled in the coffee trolley. She had come awake soon after 07.30. The three sleeping pills had seen her through the night, and now awake, she was no longer apprehensive. Archer would arrive. She would telephone her bank, instructing them to pay two million dollars into Archer's account. Presumably, some time in the afternoon, he would check his bank to make certain the money had arrived, then she would have Chris back! She lay dreaming for an hour, thinking of Chris, feeling his hands on her body, thinking of the moment when they would fly off together to Paradise City and this horrible nightmare would be over.

As Hinkle poured the coffee, he said, 'I trust you slept well, madame?'

She smiled.

'Pills, Hinkle.' She drew in a deep breath. 'Some time tonight he will be back! I want you to pack my things. Tomorrow, he and I will fly to Paradise City.'

'It would be as well, madame, to await Mr. Archer's arrival. I will pack this afternoon, after he has gone.'

She looked sharply at him.

'Nothing can go wrong! The money is ready! Mr Grenville will be back tonight!'

'Shall I draw your bath, madame, or would you prefer to rest awhile?'

'I'll have my bath now.'

There was a clouded expression on Hinkle's face that made her feel uneasy. She watched him go to the bathroom. Having started the mixer, he came from the bathroom and prepared to leave the room.

'Hinkle! Is there something wrong? Something you haven't told me about?'

'There are things I have to attend to, madame,' Hinkle said quietly. 'Excuse me,' and he left the room.

Helga frowned. There were moments like this when

Hinkle exasperated her. Could something be wrong? She got out of bed and went into the bathroom. She remembered what Hinkle had said: *a woman faced with a difficult problem is always at her best, when looking her best.* She put on a peach-coloured trouser suit, regarded herself in the full-length mirror, nodded, then walked out onto the terrace.

The time was 09.45. Two more hours to wait!

As she sat down, feeling the morning sun on her face, Hinkle appeared. She was startled to see he was no longer wearing his white coat. He was dressed in a dark-blue suit with a sober blue tie. He came towards her, carrying a large orange-coloured envelope.

'Madame Rolfe,' he said quietly, 'I wish to talk to you: not as your servant, but as someone who wishes you well and, if I may say so, as a friend.'

Helga stared at him.

'What is it? Why are you dressed like this?'

'If you find you can't accept what I am about to tell you,' Hinkle said, 'it is my intention to leave immediately.' Without asking her permission, he pulled up a chair and sat down. This was something he had never done before, and Helga could only stare at him.

'Leave? I – I thought you understood, Hinkle.'

'It is you who must understand,' Hinkle said, regarding her. 'For you to understand, I must ask you to listen to what I have to say without interruption, and then, of course, you are at liberty to accept or reject what I am about to tell you.'

Helga felt a sudden cold chill run up her spine. She had a presentiment of disaster.

'I find all this most odd, Hinkle, but what have you to say?'

'I have a niece, madame; the daughter of my sister. Some fifteen years ago, she married a young Frenchman, Jean Faucon, and they settled in Paris. Faucon was a police officer. Soon after they married, he transferred to Interpol. Over the years, he has had an excellent career, and at this moment, he is an assistant commissioner. I regret to tell you, madame, when I met Mr. Grenville, I had serious doubts about him. Yesterday, I telephoned my nephew-in-law and asked him if Mr. Grenville was known to Interpol.'

Helga's face went white.

'How dare you do such a thing!' she rasped. 'You are out of your mind with jealousy! I won't listen to another word!'

Hinkle regarded her sadly.

'You will listen to what I have to say, madame. I have all the proof you need to convince you that what I am about to tell you is fact. Last night, a police officer arrived with Mr. Grenville's police dossier which, as a very special favour, my nephew-in-law had had flown to Geneva. It is a photocopy. Mr. Grenville is wanted by the German police on three charges of bigamy.'

Helga shrivelled. She put her hands to her face while she stared at Hinkle.

'Bigamy?' Her voice was husky.

'Yes, madame. According to the dossier, Mr. Grenville appears to prey on elderly women. His method appears to be to find some rich, lonely woman, marry her, live on her until he becomes bored with her, and then leave her to repeat the operation with some other lonely woman.'

'I can't believe it!' Helga cried, her voice shrill. 'I won't believe it! I won't listen to you!'

Relentlessly, Hinkle continued, 'The kidnapping was an obvious fake. The police have established that only two days ago, Mr. Grenville and Mr. Archer were seen together in your Rolls. There is no question about that. Mr. Archer gave the policeman his card, and Mr. Grenville showed the policeman his passport. I have listened to the tape recording I made of your interview with Mr. Archer, and Mr. Archer said he hadn't met Mr. Grenville, yet the day before, he was in your car with Mr. Grenville.'

Helga closed her eyes and her hands turned into fists.

'The details are here in this dossier.'

'Bigamy!' The word came from her in a wild cry. 'The sonofabitch wanted me to marry him!'

Hinkle watched her sadly. Then he saw a sudden change in her. She stiffened, and her eyes snapped open. Her face became a mask of marble, and her eyes turned into blue points of steel.

Getting to her feet, she began to pace the terrace. Hinkle sat still, looking down at his freckled hands. After some minutes, she came to him.

'Women are fools, aren't they, Hinkle?' She put her hand on his shoulder. 'Will you please put on your white coat?'

Hinkle got to his feet.

'It will be a pleasure, madame.'

She regarded him.

'In an hour, Archer will be arriving. Send him to me. I will deal with him.'

The steely note in her voice was reassuring to Hinkle.

'Very well, madame.'

When he left the terrace, Helga, smouldering with fury, took the papers from the orange envelope and began to read them.

CHAPTER EIGHT

ARCHER lay in bed in the cramped bedroom of the rented villa. He had scarcely slept that night. It had been a shock to realize that he was now in the hands of the Mafia, and that Grenville was in an even more precarious situation. Archer now wished desperately that he hadn't embarked on this kidnap plan. The idea of getting two million dollars from Helga had dulled his caution. He ran his fingers through his thinning hair. He told himself that he had been utterly reckless to have ever mixed himself up with a man like Moses Seigal, and out of his mind to have gone to a thug like Bernie with his story of a faked kidnapping.

He cringed at the thought of having to tell Helga the ransom money now would be increased to ten million dollars. How would she react? She could, of course, afford to pay, but would her fascination for Grenville run to such a sum? Suppose she tried to bluff? Suppose she even refused? Suppose these thugs cut off Grenville's ear and forced him (Archer) to deliver it to Helga?

This was unthinkable! It mustn't happen! He must convince her she had to pay!

He longed to snatch up his suitcase, desert Grenville, and leave Switzerland, then go to England, but Bernie had guessed he might bolt. Without his passport, he couldn't leave!

He twisted and turned in the bed, sweat beading his face. Now, if he could trust Bernie, he would get only five hundred thousand dollars. A million seemed so safe, but five hundred thousand would cut his plans by half. But suppose, when Helga paid, Bernie laughed at him and gave him nothing? This was a serious possibility!

His heart thumping sluggishly, Archer heaved himself out of bed and went into the bathroom. As he shaved, he regarded himself in the mirror. His fat heavy face was waxy white and dark rings were around his eyes from lack of sleep. His look of despair and defeat, like the mark of a leper, was there for anyone to see.

He hunted for a clean shirt, finally finding one in his suitcase: a shirt with a frayed collar and a button missing from one of the cuffs. He felt old and shabby, but he must, he told himself, pull himself together. He mustn't let Helga get a hint that he was in trouble. He knew her so well. She was utterly ruthless, once she knew she had the advantage.

Then he did something he had never done before at this hour in the morning. He went to the closet and took out the bottle of whisky. He poured a stiff drink and tossed it down, then he poured another, and carrying the glass, he sat down, feeling the whisky moving through him, strengthening him.

The second drink made him slightly drunk, but at least, he felt much more confident.

At 10.15 the telephone bell rang.

It was Bernie.

'In a few minutes, Mr. Archer, you will be negotiating on my behalf with the Rolfe woman. I am relying on you. Do you anticipate trouble?'

'I don't know. She is difficult.'

'It occurred to me that it would be an idea if Mr. Grenville spoke to her. He is a little nervous, and he could be very convincing. In fact, Mr. Archer, he appears very concerned about losing an ear. So I suggest you time your arrival at her villa at exactly eleven o'clock, then in half an hour, I will get Mr. Grenville to the telephone. It could make the deal easier for you.'

Archer hesitated, then realizing he would need all the help he could get, said, 'Yes, do that.'

'Then at eleven-thirty, Mr. Grenville will call her,' and Bernie hung up.

Archer began to pace up and down in the small living-room. If Grenville talked as hysterically as he had done the previous day on the telephone, Archer felt there was every possibility that Helga's resistance to the new demand would be demolished, always providing she was as in love with Grenville as Grenville claimed. Archer began to be more hopeful that she would pay, but he was far from hopeful that Bernie would give him anything, once the transaction was over.

Bernie had asked for bearer bonds. Bolstered by the whisky, Archer suddenly smiled. No! He wouldn't ask Helga for bearer bonds. The money would have to be paid into his own numbered account where Bernie couldn't get his hands on it! That was the way to handle it! By doing this, he had Bernie under control. Bernie wouldn't dare do anything to him as long as the money was in his (Archer's) account. He would be in a strong position to deal with Bernie. Ten million dollars! He would give Bernie five and keep five for himself. Magnanimously, he decided to give Grenville a million from his own share.

Archer gave a drunken little chuckle. He looked at his watch. It was time to go. Lurching a little, he left the villa and got into the Mercedes. By the time he reached Villa Helios, he was comparatively sober, and much less confident. Leaving the Mercedes at the bottom of the drive, he walked up to the front door and thumbed the bell.

There was a long pause, then the front door opened, and Hinkle surveyed him.

'Hello, Hinkle?' Archer said, forcing a broad smile, 'I believe Madame Rolfe is expecting me.'

'That is correct,' Hinkle said stiffly. 'I will show you the way.'

Following Hinkle's broad back, Archer walked through the living-room and out onto the terrace.

Helga, wearing dark sun goggles, lay on a sun chair, a glass of vodka martini on a table by her side.

'Mr. Archer, madame,' Hinkle announced.

Without looking round, Helga waved to an upright chair. Hinkle pushed the chair forward so that when Archer sat down, he would be facing Helga, with the sun in his eyes.

'You may leave us, Hinkle,' Helga said.

'Yes, madame,' and Hinkle went away.

'Well, Helga,' Archer said, and turning the chair so the sun wasn't in his eyes, sat down. 'You look splendid as usual.'

The darkness of her sun goggles bothered him. Her eyes, which he knew from long experience, revealed her feelings, were now masked to him.

She said nothing, nor did she move. Her hands rested in her lap. She seemed completely relaxed.

Archer cleared his throat.

'I have bad news, Helga,' he began. 'First I want you to understand that I am representing my client, and what I have to say to you is entirely on his instructions.' He waited, but as she remained silent, he went on, 'My client has now realized how very wealthy you are. One of his Mafia friends has just been paid seven million dollars for returning a kidnap victim. My client has raised the ransom price. He wants ten million dollars for Grenville's return.'

Helga remained still and silent. After a long pause, Archer, sweating, asked uneasily, 'Did you hear what I said?'

'I'm not deaf,' Helga said, and the steel in her voice startled him.

'Well, there it is. I assure you this is not of my making. What do you say? Are you willing to pay ten million dollars to get Grenville back?'

Helga moved in her chair: the movements of a cat stretching.

'How much of this money goes to you?' she asked.

'That is nothing to do with you!' Archer snapped. 'Is it yes or no?'

She turned her head, and he could feel she was staring at him, but behind the dark sun goggles she was anonymous.

'And suppose it is no?'

So she was going to bluff, and his uneasiness increased.

'That is up to you,' he said. 'Grenville is in the hands of vicious people. I regret having to deal with them. If you refuse to pay the ransom, they will cut off one of his ears, and will force me to deliver it to you. This is a terrible situation for me. I am in the same trap as Grenville. I assure you, Helga, if you want him back, you must pay.'

Still regarding him from behind the shield of her sun goggles, she said, 'You are in a trap?'

'I've explained that to you. I didn't know I was dealing with the Mafia,' Archer said. 'They are utterly ruthless. I am forced to do what they tell me.'

'How sad for you,' Helga said.

He flushed.

'We are wasting time! What is it to be? Yes or no?'

Again Helga moved like a cat stretching, then she reached for her drink and finished it.

'What do you know of a man called Timothy Wilson?' she asked.

Startled, Archer stared at her.

'Timothy Wilson? I am not interested in any Timothy Wilsons! I am asking you: is it yes or no?'

Helga reached for a cigarette and lit it.

'There was a time when I thought you had brains, were shrewd and clever. Since you turned embezzler, forger, blackmailer, and now a creature of the Mafia, I have come to regard you as beyond contempt.'

Archer clenched his fists.

'Now listen to me! I have had enough of your insults! If you want your lover back, you will arrange to pay ten million dollars into an account in Geneva! If you don't want him back, then say so!'

Helga's lips moved into a bitter smile.

'Poor, shabby Archer,' she said. 'How stupid can you be! Let me tell you about Timothy Wilson. His father was a badly paid golf pro who, at least, taught his son to play good golf. This boy had looks, and a burning ambition. Although he claims to have gone to Eton and Cambridge, actually he left home when he was sixteen, and went to Paris as an apprentice at the Crillion Hotel. There he learned French, but his work was unsatisfactory. He then went to Italy, where he was a waiter in a small restaurant in Milan, but he did learn

Italian. His work was never satisfactory. His main interest in life was women. From Italy, he went to Germany, and became a waiter at the Adlon Hotel, and learned German. A rich, elderly woman fell for him, and offered him marriage. They married, and for two years he lived on her, doing nothing, then he got bored with her. He found another rich old woman who offered marriage, and he married her. Again he tired of her demands, and married yet another rich old woman. Before all this happened, Timothy Wilson changed his name to Christopher Grenville.'

Archer felt a shock run through him. He began to say something, but Helga went on, her voice steely, cutting him short. 'I have Grenville's or Wilson's police dossier,' she said. 'He is wanted by the German police for bigamy.'

As Archer slumped down in his chair, sweat beading his face, he heard the telephone bell ring in the living-room.

'Do you still like the look of your four aces?' Helga asked. 'That was what you said? You held the four aces?'

Hinkle came out onto the terrace.

'Excuse me, madame, Mr. Grenville is on the telephone, asking to speak to you.'

As Helga shook her hed, Archer's last shred of hope vanished.

'I have no wish to speak to him,' she said.

'Very well, madame.' Hinkle returned to the living-room. In the heavy silence that followed, Archer heard Hinkle say, 'Madame has no wish to speak to you.'

Then Helga took off her sun goggles and stared directly at Archer. The blazing fury in her eyes frightened him.

'Get out! I don't believe one word you have said to me! The Mafia! That is a crude joke! You and this despicable bigamist dreamed up this ridiculous plot to get money from me! You told me you didn't know him, you cheap liar! I have police proof that you two have been seen together! Get out of my sight! You haven't even the intelligence to bluff! Go away!'

Archer looked as if he were about to have a heart attack. He clawed at his collar as he struggled to breathe.

Helga watched him, her face a stone mask.

Finally, gasping, Archer said, 'Helga, you must listen to me! You must believe me! I will tell you the truth. Grenville and I did concoct this plan for you to think he had been kidnapped. I had a shady contact in Geneva, and stupidly, I asked him to get me two reliable men to fake the kidnapping. I swear I am telling you the truth! Once they got Grenville, it turned into a genuine kidnapping. They have taken my passport! They forced me to come to you. Doesn't Grenville mean anything to you?' He waved his hands in despair. 'You loved him! Unless you pay this money, they will disfigure him! They are utterly ruthless and vicious! Helga, you must do something to help him!'

Helga lit another cigarette, and Archer saw her hands were steady.

'Yes, I did love him,' she said quietly, 'but now that is finished. How could any woman continue to love a cheat and a liar: a man so degraded, he will marry time and again, old women, so he can live in luxury?' Her voice turned strident and leaning forward, her face alight with fury, she screamed at him, 'I don't believe one word of your Mafia lies! You were always a cheap bluffer! Get out! You can consider yourself lucky I don't hand you and your bigamist over to the police, but I warn you, if you ever come near me again, you will regret it! Now get out!'

Hinkle appeared on the terrace, and touched Archer on his shoulder.

Almost crying, Archer staggered to his feet.

'Helga! I swear I am telling you the truth!' he cried. 'These people . . .'

With surprising strength, Hinkle caught hold of Archer's arm, turned him and pushed him off the terrace and to the front door.

Archer stumbled down the drive and slumped into his car. Hinkle watched him drive away, then returned to the terrace.

Her fists clenched, her lips trembling, Helga said shakily, 'Pack, Hinkle. I will leave tomorrow.'

'That would be wise, madame.'

He gave her a brief glance, his expression sad, then he went into her bedroom and took her suitcases from the closet.

Helga put her hand across her eyes. Timothy Wilson! Not only a cheat, but a bigamist! And how she had loved him! A man, according to the police, who preyed on old women! She didn't believe a word Archer had said about the Mafia. He had tried to bluff her in the past, and she had called his bluff. He and Grenville had hoped this stupid Mafia threat would have frightened her to pay. To hell with both of them!

She drew in a long deep breath. Men seemed fatal to her. Somehow, she must rid herself of this nagging sexual urge that continually got her into trouble. She closed her eyes, and her mind re-created those marvellous moments when she had been lying in Chris's arms. Had he been a thief, or even a murderer, she could have forgiven him, but being a despicable calculating bigamist . . . no!

She got to her feet, and went to her bedroom where Hinkle was carefully packing her clothes.

'It's a mess, isn't it, Hinkle? she said, forcing a smile. 'I'll be glad to leave.' She touched his arm. 'Thank you for being such a good and loyal friend to me.'

Hinkle looked sadly at her.

'You have courage, madame, and with courage, there can be no defeat.'

As Archer drove back to Paradiso, he felt like a panic-trapped mouse. As Helga had refused to speak to Grenville, Bernie would have guessed she wouldn't pay the ransom. What would Bernie do? He would either turn Grenville free or become vicious.

Whatever he did, Archer wanted no part of it. He decided he would pick up his suitcase and drive fast to Geneva. He would tell the U.S. Consulate that he had lost his passport.

He would tell them he had urgent business in England. He would show them his old business card. They would have to help him!

He wished he had put his suitcase in the boot of the Mercedes, instead of leaving it in the rented villa. The suitcase contained all his few belongings, and he had to have it! If he hurried, he would still have time to collect it and be on his way before Bernie began to look for him.

The heavy lakeside traffic forced him to drive at a crawl, and by the time he reached the rented villa, he was soggy with sweat. Leaving his car, he hurried up the path and entered the villa. His suitcase was in the lobby where he had left it. As he reached for it, Bernie came from the living-room. This wasn't the smiling, oily-looking Bernie he had dealt with before: this was an alarming-looking thug whose little eyes glittered with rage.

'Come in here!' Bernie snarled. 'What happened? Why didn't she speak to him?'

His heart thumping, his face white, Archer walked unsteadily into the living-room.

'She won't pay.'

Bernie spat on the carpet.

'She will!' He turned on Archer, and shouted in a voice congested with fury, 'You fat, useless fink! I'll show you how to handle her! Come with me!'

His vicious fury horrified Archer, who took a hasty step back.

'Come with me!' Bernie snarled, and leaving the villa, he walked down the path and got into Archer's car. Archer hesitated, then defeated, knowing there was nothing he could do but obey, he picked up his suitcase and joined Bernie in the car.

Saying nothing, his bearded face contorted with vicious rage, Bernie drove to Lucky's store.

'Open the gates!'

With some trouble, because he was shaking, Archer opened the gates, and Bernie drove the car into the yard.

'Come!'

He led the way up into the barn, up the stairs, and into the big room. Archer followed.

Grenville, in need of a shave, looking utterly demoralized, was sitting in one of the armchairs. Seeing Archer, he jumped to his feet.

158

'What went wrong?' he demanded wildly. 'Why wouldn't she speak to me?'

'I wish I had never set eyes on you,' Archer said, and feeling his legs becoming unsteady, he dropped into a chair. 'You ask why she didn't speak to you? Because you are a bigamist! If I had known you were wanted by the police for bigamy, I wouldn't have touched you! Why didn't you tell me – damn you!'

Grenville's face turned the colour of tallow.

'Does she know?'

'She knows! She has a copy of your German police dossier! God knows how she got it, but she now has proof you are Timothy Wilson and an utter fake! She knows you married three old women for gain, and these three old women are still living!'

'God!' Grenville looked frantically around the room. 'I've got to get away! She will tell the police!'

Listening to all this, Bernie suddenly broke in. 'You two goddamn amateurs! If you imagine I am going to pass up ten million dollars, you have another think coming! I'm going to see just how tough this bitch is!'

He went to the door and whistled.

Segetti and Belmont, who had been in the barn, came quickly up the stairs and entered the room.

'She won't pay,' Bernie said to them. 'Now we must soften her.' He pointed to Grenville. 'Cut his ear off!' Then swinging around and glaring at Archer, he went on, 'You will take his ear, bleeding to her, and if she doesn't pay, you will take his other ear, and if she doesn't pay, you will take every day, one of his fingers until she does pay!'

Almost sick with horror, Archer said, 'You must listen to me! If he had been a thief, a forger, anything but a bigamist, she would have forgiven him and paid. Don't you understand? He promised to marry her, and now, she finds he is a bigamist! She will never pay!'

Bernie spat on the floor.

'We can try. Cut his ear off, Jacques!'

Belmont's hand went behind him. He produced a long, razor sharp knife. He looked at Segetti, who nodded and took from his hip-pocket a leather-covered cosh.

'Just a tap on your head, Mr. Grenville,' Bernie said, smiling evilly. 'You won't feel much. Jacques is an expert. Maybe a little sore later, but it is worth a try.'

Grenville backed away, while Archer, shocked, hid his face in his hands.

Then Grenville said hoarsely, 'Wait! Listen to me! I can tell you how you can get fifteen million dollars from her! I know her – you don't! Fifteen million, and it is certain money!'

Bernie lifted his hand, stopping Segetti as he moved towards Grenville.

'She hates violence,' Grenville said, sweat running down his face. 'Our mistake was sending Archer to talk to her. You should have gone. You would have convinced her, but it is now too late to use me as a lever, but I have thought of another lever, but you will have to talk to her.'

Bernie nodded.

'Okay. I will talk to her . . . about what?'

Archer was staring at Grenville. Belmont, fingering his knife, and Segetti tapping the palm of his hand with his cosh, were also staring at Grenville.

'We should have thought of this before,' Grenville said. 'We wouldn't have had all this trouble. It's so easy . . . so simple.'

Bernie walked up to him and dug his forefinger into Grenville's chest

'What is so easy . . . so simple?' he demanded, a snarl in his voice.

Grenville told him.

Just after 08.15, Helga came awake from a drugged sleep. She stretched, and then looked around the luxurious bedroom. She had no regrets, leaving this room for good. The villa now held too many unhappy memories. She thought of Chris, and was thankful she could think of him without heartache. In a few weeks, she assured herself, she would have forgotten him. He would become yet another shadowy man in her past.

How careful, she thought, one had to be when one thinks one is in love. What is love? She had to admit that she had never known the real meaning of love. It was something, she now suspected, she would never know. Love was illusive. So many men and women believed they were in love, and then found, one day, that love meant nothing, and that they had become strangers. And yet, she knew, there were as many men and women who had discovered that love meant a solid background to their lives. To her, love meant sexual excitement. Sex! This was the curse that influenced her life. She had really believed she had been in love with Chris, but when Hinkle had told her that this handsome, suave man was not only a bigamist, but a calculating cheat, her love for him had abruptly ceased, like the switching off of a light.

In a few hours, she would be at the Geneva airport, leaving Hinkle to supervise the sale of the villa and the furniture. She would fly to Paradise City and take up her dreary, lonely life, commuting to New York for equally dreary board meetings, working with Loman and Winborn. This seemed now to be the pattern of her future life. Next June, she would be forty-five!

She looked at the bedside clock. The time was 08.40. Hinkle was late! Well, never mind, she wasn't desperate for coffee. He had had a hard day packing, and clearing her personal things from her closets. He had probably overslept.

She closed her eyes and let herself drift into a doze, then came awake later with a little start, to see it was 09.10.

No Hinkle?

She got out of bed, went into the bathroom and took a shower. Putting on a wrap, she went into the living-room. The french windows were closed. Puzzled, she threw them open, and then went to the front door which she found unlocked. She opened the door and looked down the short drive to the main road.

It occurred to her that Hinkle had gone down to Castagnola village for fresh milk, and she shrugged. This had never happened before, but then for all she knew, the milk had never turned sour before, but she had an uneasy feeling, so she went into the kitchen and opened the refrigerator door. She saw there were three cartons of milk on the shelf.

She experienced a sudden clutch of fear. Was Hinkle ill? Had he had a heart attack after his exertions the previous day? She went quickly to her bedroom and dressed, putting on a red trouser suit. She was dressed in less than three minutes, then she ran down the long corridor that led to Hinkle's room. She rapped loudly on the door, waited, her heart thudding, then rapped again. Silence greeted her. Bracing herself, she turned the door handle and opened the door.

Peering into the room, she saw the bed had been made, the room was in immaculate order, but no Hinkle.

Panic now nibbling at her, she ran back along the corridor and opening the front door, she went to the garage. Hinkle's VW stood beside the Carmague Rolls. So he hadn't gone down to the village! Then where was he?

Had he gone into the garden, and there had a heart attack? She ran down the steep steps, looking to right and left, until she reached the gate, leading to the main road. The gate was locked. Satisfied that Hinkle was not in the garden, she took the chair lift back to the villa.

Where was Hinkle?

It was during the short run up to villa in the chair lift that Helga realized what this loyal servant really meant to her. She knew him to be her only true friend. Now, his absence frightened her. Had he decided to leave her? No! He would never do such a thing without telling her first! Then what had happened? Where was he?

The little cabin of the chair lift came to rest, and she got out and walked across the terrace into the living-room, wondering if she should call the police, then she came to an abrupt stop.

Sitting in a lounging chair, a cigarette hanging from his lips was a short, squat man with a heavy black beard, flat features and small glittering black eyes. He was wearing a dirty blue polo neck sweater and grey trousers on which were several oil stains. He held in his lap an electric hand drill which he had plugged into a nearby socket.

The sight of this evil-looking man sent shock through Helga, turning her cold. She realized that she was alone with him. There was no Hinkle to protect her, but the steel in her made an effort to assert itself, and she said, her voice steady, 'What are you doing here?'

Bernie grinned at her. He switched on the drill and leaning forward, bored a hole in the antique coffee table by him. Having made the hole, he levered out the drill and then bored another hole. Then he switched off the drill.

'Handy tool, isn't it, lady?' he said.

Helga drew in a shuddering breath.

'What do you want?' she asked, not moving.

'I thought it was time, lady, to talk to you,' Bernie said. 'That fink Archer didn't seem able to convince you that we mean business. From what he tells me, your lover boy now doesn't mean a thing to you. I was going to cut off his ears, but he sold me another idea.' He leaned forward and bored another hole in the table.

So Archer hadn't been bluffing! This terrifying creature must be a mafisto, Helga thought. Looking at him, she realized he was far too vicious and ruthless for her to attempt to handle.

'What do you want?' This time her voice was unsteady.

He levered the drill bit free.

'Fifteen million dollars, lady, in bearer bonds.' Then he leaned forward, and with a snarl in his voice, he went on, 'I have your servant, Hinkle. Grenville said Hinkle was important to you. Is he?'

Helga felt faint. Moving unsteadily, she dropped into a chair.

'Where is he?'

'You'll see. You and I are going to him now.' Bernie bored yet another hole in the table. 'You will see how useful this tool is, lady. Unless you pay up, I'll give you a little exhibition that will make you change your mind.' He got to his feet. 'Let's go.'

'I'm not going with you!'

Bernie regarded her evilly.

'I said let's go, and listen, lady, have you ever thought what happens when a fink gets a drill bit like this through both his kneecaps? You play along with me, lady, or your fink servant won't walk again.'

Helga felt the blood drain from her face. She had always had a horror of violence, and this obscene threat nearly turned her sick . . . and to Hinkle!

'I'll pay.' She got unsteadily to her feet. 'I'll call my bank now.'

Bernie studied her, nodded and grinned.

'That's being sensible, but no tricks. Go ahead and fix it. I want the bonds here by tomorrow morning or else this drill goes into action.'

Shaking, Helga went to the telephone and picked up the receiver.

'That will be quite unnecessary, madame,' Hinkle said in his fruity, bishop's voice.

Helga spun around.

Standing in the french windows, flanked on either side by two tall, heavily-built men, both with automatic pistols in their hands, was Hinkle: admittedly an unshaven, crumpled-looking Hinkle, but still, Hinkle.

Bernie started to his feet, dropping the drill, as one of the big men moved over to him.

'Hello, Bernie,' the man said. 'You have had a long run, now it's our turn. Come on.'

Bernie eyed the gun, then shrugged.

'You can't pin anything on me, Bazzi,' he snarled, 'and you know it.'

The big man smiled.

'We can always try, Bernie. Let's go.'

Bernie glared at Hinkle, then moved across the living-room. The two police officers followed. The front door slammed. A car started up and drove away.

Hinkle said, 'I must ask you to excuse me, madame. I am looking dishevelled. If you would be kind enough to give me a few moments, I will get you some coffee.'

Tears began to run down Helga's face. She went to him, and putting her arms around him, she hugged him.

'Oh, Hinkle! I was so frightened! If they had done anything dreadful to you . . .'

'Madame!' Hinkle's voice was sharp. 'You must excuse me for a few minutes,' and giving her a fatherly pat on her shoulder, he disengaged himself and walked fast to his quarters.

Helga dropped into a chair and continued to cry.

She had stopped crying, and was in control of herself, when Hinkle, immaculate, pushed in the coffee trolley.

'I suggest a little cognac mixed with the coffee, madame,' he said. 'It is good for the nerves.'

Her lips trembling, she forced a smile.

'You think of everything, Hinkle, but I don't drink a thing unless you join me, and please sit down.'

Hinkle raised his eyebrows.

'I mean it!' Helga said sharply.

'Very well, madame. I will get a second cup.'

There was a pause, then Hinkle returned, carrying a cup and saucer. He poured coffee into the two cups, added the cognac, then sat down, opposite Helga.

'Madame, I have to apologize,' he said. 'I have exposed you to a terrible experience, but I assure you, the police insisted it was the only way to trap these ruffians.'

Helga sipped her coffee. Hinkle's quiet presence had a soothing effect on her.

'Tell me, Hinkle. I want to know what happened.'

'Of course, madame. As you are aware, I telephoned my nephew-in-law, Jean Faucon, about Mr. Grenville. What you didn't know is that I told Faucon about the whole situation, and that Mr. Grenville had been supposedly kidnapped and that Mr. Archer was demanding a two million dollar ransom. Faucon alerted the Swiss police. Inspector Bazzi had had this villa watched now for the past two days. He wanted to find out where Mr. Grenville and Mr. Archer were hiding. When I got rid of Mr. Archer, a police officer followed him to a rented villa in Paradiso, and this man

Bernie appeared. Apparently, Bernie is well known to the police, but he has been astute enough not to give them any evidence to arrest him. The police followed Mr. Archer and Bernie to a small shop in Lugano and a watch was kept. The Swiss police are patient. They waited. Apparently, Bernie decided, as you appeared to have lost interest in Mr. Grenville, to kidnap me. This move was unforeseen by the police, but as our villa was under guard, there was no reason for alarm.

'This morning, I opened the front door, as is my custom, and was seized by two ruffians who forced me into a car, and drove me to this shop which has a barn at the back. There, I found Mr. Grenville and Mr. Archer and this evil man, Bernie. Still the police waited. Bernie left and came here to threaten you. As soon as he had gone, the police, under the direction of Inspector Bazzi, arrested Mr. Grenville and Mr. Archer and the two ruffians. Inspector Bazzi and I then drove here and were in time to hear Bernie threatening you.' Hinkle paused, then went on. 'That is the story, madame. I regret that you have been subjected to such an alarming experience, and that this evil man should have ruined such a nice table.'

'I don't give a damn about the table,' Helga said. 'I'm only so thankful I have you back.'

'Thank you, madame.' Hinkle finished his coffee. 'The whole affair will be handled with the utmost discretion. Inspector Bazzi tells me that Mr. Grenville will be sent back to Germany to face bigamy charges. Bernie, and his two ruffians will be charged with receiving stolen property. The police searched Bernie's apartment, and it contains a considerable amount of stolen property. Inspector Bazzi understands that it would be better to drop the kidnapping charge, so you will not be involved.'

'And Archer?' Helga asked.

'Mr. Archer, of course, presents a problem. I found Inspector Bazzi most understanding. I felt sure you would not wish to prosecute Mr. Archer as Mr. Rolfe refrained from prosecuting him. If he were prosecuted, he could make difficulties.' Hinkle's voice went down a tone to show his disapproval. 'It has been arranged that Mr. Archer should be deported from Switzerland, and not allowed to return. In the circumstances, and to avoid charging him, it seems the best course.'

Helga looked at him. She told herself this kindly man must have known for some time that at one time she had been Archer's mistress. Probably, her husband had told him. How wise Hinkle was! She was sure that if Archer were charged, he would try, and probably succeed, in telling the world, through the press, that in the past, the fabulous, wealthy Mrs. Rolfe use to lie on his office floor, while he serviced her.

'Yes,' she said, and looked away. 'So it is over.'

'Yes, madame. Now, there are things to do. You will be catching the three o'clock flight to New York.' He got to his feet. 'I have to complete the packing.' As he picked up the tray, he paused, then said, 'May I suggest, madame, in the future, you should get your values right. I am certainly not worth fifteen million dollars.' His kindly, fat face lit up with a warm smile, 'But I thank you.'

Leaving her, he walked into the kitchen.

To Archer's surprise, Inspector Bazzi of the Ticino police turned out to be genial and talkative, in spite of his heavy features, his thin mouth and his small cop's eyes.

Smiling affably, he told Archer he was going to escort him personally to the Geneva airport, and to see him safely on the London flight. While driving Archer to the airport, he talked of his wife and son, and the holiday he was taking in Nice at the end of the month. Unless one had known, Archer thought, one would never guess this massively-built man at his side, was a police officer.

Utterly relieved that he wasn't to be arrested, but merely deported, Archer regained some of his bounce. He gave Bazzi the names of several cheap, but good restaurants in the Nice neighbourhood, and also recommended two modest, but good hotels. Bazzi thanked him, and said he would re-member Archer's suggestions.

Together, they walked into the airport lobby, and Archer parted with his shabby suitcase and had his flight ticket checked. The formalities over, the two men passed through the customs. The two customs officers eyed Archer, shook hands with Bazzi and waved them through. Bazzi then went with Archer into the flight take-off lounge.

'There will be a delay,' Bazzi said. 'The London flight will be late.'

'Everything to do with England is late these days,' Archer said sourly.

The two men settled themselves on one of the benches that overlooked the tarmac where several aircraft were lined up.

'Just an official word, Mr. Archer,' Bazzi said with his genial smile. 'Please don't attempt to return to Switzerland. That is understood, isn't it?'

'Yes.'

'Good.' Bazzi regarded him. 'I must say, Mr. Archer, you are a very fortunate man. Had Madame Rolfe brought charges against you, you would have spent many disagreeable years in one of our jails.'

Archer nodded.

'She had her reasons,' he said.

'The very rich always have reasons.' Bazzi shrugged. 'So, you are going to London. Would it be inquisitive to ask what you will do there, Mr. Archer?'

The question was put in a most friendly way, and Archer wished he could answer truthfully.

'What shall I do?' he repeated, thinking, 'What shall I do? How I wish I knew!' He had several contacts in London, but they were all, more or less, in the same depressing boat as himself: fringe people, feverishly hunting for quick money. Perhaps, if he were lucky, one of them could use his services and his brains for a small fee: if he were lucky, but he wasn't going to tell Bazzi this. 'You have no idea, Inspector, of the opportunities there are in England. There are interesting loans to be floated, Arab money anxious to be invested, property developers looking for new outlets ... many, many opportunities for a man of my experience.'

Bazzi eyed him thoughtfully, then smiled.

'I was under the impression, Mr. Archer, that England, at this moment, is suffering from some kind of depression.'

Archer waved his hand airily.

'That is mere newspaper talk. You should never believe what you read in the papers. You would be surprised how much hidden wealth still remains in England.'

'Is that so?'

'Quite right. Oh, I know there is a lot of talk about England's troubles. What country doesn't have troubles, and strikes?' Archer wagged his head. 'But I assure you, I shall have no difficulty.'

There was a slight commotion which caused both men to look up. Two press photographers were hovering, then Helga, looking radiant, carrying a small bag and her coat, swept through the lounge and into the V.I.P. room.

'Ah, Mrs. Rolfe herself!' Bazzi said. 'A fine-looking woman.'

Archer became deflated. So, Helga had already forgotten Grenville, he thought. She couldn't look so radiant, so happy if she were grieving. What a bitch!

If his kidnap plan had succeeded, he too would have been able to walk into the V.I.P. lounge, and be fawned over by stewards. Now, here he was, under police escort, flying tourist-class to London, not knowing how long his money would last before he found some shady promoter with a proposition.

'A fine-looking woman,' Bazzi repeated. 'At one time, I understand, Mr. Archer, you had the privilege of working with her.'

Archer wasn't listening. He was regarding a tall, well-built man in his early fifties who had just entered the lounge. This man was immaculately dressed, and exuded money and power. His lean, strong face with a cleft chin, china blue eyes, and a grey clipped moustache gave him an impressive, eye-catching appearance.

Bazzi, following Archer's glance, said, 'Ah! That is Monsieur Henri de Villiers: one of the richest and most important industrialists of France. There are rumours that he will be the next French Ambassador to the United States.'

Already, the two photographers were letting off their flash-lights. De Villiers paused, gave a charming smile, before an air hostess ushered him into the V.I.P. lounge.

Archer heaved a sigh.

With a million dollars, he too could have been as impressive as this man, he thought.

The New York flight was announced.

'There they go,' Bazzi said, turning to look down on the tarmac.

Archer saw Helga moving towards the aircraft. Behind her was de Villiers, followed by two other people. Archer watched Helga's easy stride; then half-way to the aircraft, she dropped something white which could have been a handkerchief, but Archer was too far away to be sure. De Villiers picked it up, and lengthening his stride, gave it to Helga. Archer watched her pause and look up at this imposing man, and then give him a flashing smile. They exchanged words, then de Villiers took her small bag, and together, they walked to the aircraft.

Bazzi chuckled.

'That, I think, was fast work,' he said.

'She has always worked fast, and always will,' Archer said sourly, then hearing his London flight called, he got to his feet.

'Good-bye, Mr. Archer.' Bazzi shook hands. 'Good luck.'

Knowing he would need all the luck in the world, Archer thanked him.

THE END

>>> If you've enjoyed this book and would like to discover more great vintage crime and thriller titles, as well as the most exciting crime and thriller authors writing today, visit: >>>

The Murder Room
Where Criminal Minds Meet

themurderroom.com

www.ingramcontent.com/pod-product-compliance
Ingram Content Group UK Ltd.
Pitfield, Milton Keynes, MK11 3LW, UK
UKHW022309280225
455674UK00004B/234

9 781471 903953